Jordan's Trials

Love Strictly Tested Book Three

by

Anna Hague

Jordan's Trials

Contact Information: info@thewildrosepress.com

Cover Art by *Diana Carlile*

The Wild Rose Press, Inc.
PO Box 708
Adams Basin, NY 14410-0708

Visit us at www.thewildrosepress.com

Publishing History
First Scarlet Rose Edition, 2020
Print ISBN 978-1-5092-2992-5
Digital ISBN 978-1-5092-2993-2

Published in the United States of America

Dedication

To my husband, who is my Jordan.

Prologue

Thunderstruck. Affected. Blown away.

Choose one or all three, but those are the words I'd use to describe the second Emma spilled red wine all over my shirt. Not because I gave a rat's ass about my shirt, but rather, when she flashed her horrified expression, she had me.

I was thirty-fuckin'-five years old, and became seventeen. This mass of curls on her head somewhere between brown and black begged for my fingers to wind themselves through the corkscrew coils.

She offered to pay for my shirt, apologizing profusely with a vein of sarcasm dotting her speech. We parted ways, but I secretly stalked her—watching her every step, gesture, and animated expression.

Even when I asked her to dance, I remained the cool in-control guy I always was. My job required such a demeanor. In the four minutes of atrocious lounge-lizard music, her web of fascination crooked its little finger luring me closer until the imminent point of no return.

She had me.

She awoke the man I was. Every ounce of me craved to bind her arms high above her head and fuck her senseless. But I'd walked away from that life—from being a Dominant. One glass of spilled wine, a dance, and I craved this smart-mouthed fiery woman to

1

submit to me, and I'd be okay this time. I'd do everything right.

Emma, she blessed me. She blessed me with her body under my command. She challenged me. She fought me. She fulfilled me.

She loved me with abandon.

My Emma. My Angel. She's my wife. She's my submissive. She's mine.

She's my world, and I'd do anything for her.

Absolutely anything…

Chapter One
Angel

"This just in. Police have identified the body of a young woman found dead in her apartment near Parker Terrace. The woman has been identified as Jessica Forner."

I dropped the plate of eggs, and among the shattered pieces, yellow goo oozed across the tile floor.

"Oh my God. Jordan, get in here!"

I tiptoed over the shards of ceramic and yolk but once clear of the mess, I sprinted to the television, grabbed the remote, and rewound the broadcast before hitting the pause button.

"What's going on?" Jordan sauntered into our living room with nothing but a towel around his narrow waist. Droplets of water clung to the ends of his hair. Normally, the sight of my husband's flat stomach and broad shoulders gave me a girly hard-on but not now—not after hearing this.

"Listen. Just listen to this." I pointed the remote to the TV and watched in horror as the words out of the anchor's mouth did not change from the first time I heard. Jessica was dead.

"That's weird." Jordan stood with his hands on his hips, but my impassioned, visceral husband showed no emotion.

"Jordan?"

"What?"

"This woman is dead and all you have to say is 'that's weird.'" I muted the broadcast which continued to a different, albeit another tragic death in the city.

I didn't recognize his face void of emotion. "She's dead, Jordan. This woman we know is dead. I mean I know the trouble she's caused, but still she's dead."

With his arms crossed across his chest, Jordan said, "I'm sorry. That's rough for her family. I'm not sure why it's newsworthy. People die every day in this city."

Who was this unfeeling man in my living room?

"I guess you weren't paying attention to the end of the story. Police are saying it's a suspicious death." I raked my hands through my hair not even feeling as my fingers ripped through the morning tangles. "They think she was murdered."

He turned and began walking toward the bedroom. "Jordan, what are you doing?"

"I'm getting ready for work."

"How can you go to work like nothing's happened?" I'd never known him to be so cold.

He turned and the towel slipped a notch lower.

"Angel, what would you have me do?" He cinched the towel tighter and leaned against the doorjamb of our bedroom. "We aren't related. We sure as hell aren't friends." The towel again slid low exposing the dark hair below his abs. "Quite honestly, this kind of solves our problem. I'm sorry she's dead, but not sorry this nightmare ends."

"Maybe you should call them." I followed him into the bedroom in time to see the towel whipped from his waist and tossed into the laundry bin. Even though his attitude seemed odd, I never tired of the view. His sculpted ass would never be the common old man ass of the masses—you know, the deflated one sliding down the back of the legs into oblivion.

"Call who?" He slathered shaving cream onto his jaw. Work day so no scruff. I loved the scruff, but watching him shave had a certain aphrodisiac effect. I know he removed the towel to tease me because we both knew a sunrise *nooner* wouldn't happen. We had less than an hour, and hell, foreplay lasted an hour. Not only was Jordan precise, but he was thorough. I suppose those qualities made him a good manager as well.

"The police."

Plop. He dropped his razor in the water and turned away from the mirror. "Angel, are you out of your fuckin' mind? Call the police and tell them the dead woman was going to release information about us that could devastate our lives? Sure, let's do that."

He retrieved the razor, shook the water from the blade, and continued to shave. "Think. Angel. Think."

All thoughts of how hot my husband was, exited from my head—replaced with *asshole* and since when did he use *fuck* when talking to me. That's my MO. "Don't you call me stupid. Maybe it wasn't my best idea, but I haven't had breakfast yet."

This time he set the razor on the sink, wiped his face with a towel, and leaned his naked body on the sink cabinet. "Despite the fact that was a stupid idea, I did not call you stupid."

Something about his exasperated tone pissed me off. I'd expected more of an "I'm sorry. I didn't mean it that way," from him. "Why are you being such a prick this morning? Somebody piss on your filet mignon or in your wine last night at dinner with the clients so special I couldn't go with you?"

When he held out his hands to me, at first I thought *why should I?* He's the one being a shit. But he knew and I knew his ice-blue eyes possessed an irresistible power over me—the sexual equivalent of offering me a s'more. No way in hell could I say no to either one.

I tried to hesitate, but one raised salacious eyebrow later, I caved into the heat of his chest and his arms enveloped my shoulders melting away my aggravation.

"I'm sorry, Angel." If he hugged any tighter, I would need a chiropractor. "That was insensitive of me. It's just…I don't know. What she was doing was unconscionable, but still, I'm sure she had people who loved her, and they're hurting."

"Jordan, you're not a mean person. I was just thrown off by your attitude toward it all." My face, always at his nipple level, rubbed the light covering of dark hair on his chest. His ocean scent reminded me he was my safe island.

When his lips went to my scalp, his voice vibrated my skin sending tingles down my back. "This has been a rough two weeks at work. I'm having to do some stuff I'm not really into doing and it's affecting me more than I realized."

I raised my gaze to meet his and my fingers skimmed along the scab over his forearm. "What's going on?"

"Things that aren't for you to worry about. It's work shit. Some parts of this job I don't like."

I could relate. Since I began freelance editing, I'd discovered some things I didn't like. For example, I'd learned a few hard lessons—like get the money before you send back the manuscript.

I trailed my fingers down his spine to his ass. His muscles clenched, and I relished my ability to arouse him with such a simple gesture. His hand grabbed mine and pressed my fingers tight against the small of his back.

"Angel, stop. As much as I would rather roll around with you, I have a meeting at…" He glanced at his phone on the sink. "Shit, in thirty minutes."

"Wouldn't be that big a deal if you missed one meeting."

"Well, since I scheduled the meeting, yes it would be bad if I didn't show up." He kissed my forehead and unwrapped my arms, holding my wrists until he pushed me into the bedroom. "Now, when I get home, we're gonna have a session. So, whatever you need to do, do it today—shower, eat a shit ton of food whatever, because it's going to be a very long night."

Ouch. That's how bad I started to throb between my legs.

Chapter Two
Jordan

I had to get my head out of my ass. Too much shit happened the last few weeks, and I'd reached my limit. I hated not telling Angel, but I didn't want her to know…ever. As well as I knew every crevasse, moan, and motion she owned, I wasn't sure how she'd react. Actually, I did. She'd be pissed as hell.

The best defense…always a good offense. I knew what we needed to release some stress. If Mark came through, then the weekend I wanted to surprise Angel with would be memorable.

I was on to Angel's tactics, but she without a doubt knew I couldn't deny her anything. I often wondered who really was the Dominant in our home.

Of course *I* was.

I was already counting the hours until I could get home and show her something new. No late nights. No client dinners. Me, my wife, and all night to hear her moans and cries of mercy. We weren't going to stop at one, or two, or even three. We might stop when the sun came up…or not.

If I could at least get a pair of underwear between us, then I was in the clear. I headed for the dresser, but a cotton swab wouldn't fit between her body and mine.

"Angel, stop. I've now got less than thirty minutes, and I'm not even dressed."

"Casual Tuesday? Jeans, college T-shirt. That doesn't take long."

"No, it's never Casual Tuesday, or Wednesday. It's not on Fridays either. I doubt Mr. Levendar would appreciate the change, and I need my job…and I like most of my job."

She snorted. "Oh come on. You're his golden boy. You make that company so much money, he'd never get rid of you." She reached to the thin black strap holding her nightgown and stared me straight in the eye as she pushed the strap to the edge of her shoulder.

"No, no, no." I pointed. "Get away from me." I turned my back to her and went straight to the closet.

"Do not follow me." I started to add, "or else you'll pay for it tonight," but knowing my wife, any comment resembling a challenge was like waving a cape at a bull.

I heard a pronounced sigh from her direction.

"Are you gonna eat the breakfast I fixed?"

I never expected her to make me breakfast, but morning after morning she did, and I appreciated every minute she spent doing something for me. From the number of people who carried paper bags every morning into our office, few ate at home I surmised. I indeed was a lucky man in more ways than one.

I bet Sabrina would make Cameron breakfast. Damn. I don't why I had thought of that. A few more weeks and that guy was out of my life…at the very least, three hours by car. His day-to-day existence would be gone, but Sabrina's *I don't know how the hell that happened* relationship with him would keep that asshole part of my life.

At least for both Sabrina's and Angel's sake, I knew Cameron wasn't abusive or mean in any way. He worshipped every woman on the planet. Me…just one.

"Anyway you can slap it on toast and wrap it in a paper towel?" I yelled from the closet.

"Okay, if I must," she yelled back.

I think the main reason she cooked breakfast on weekdays had more to do with budget than anything else. Angel believed her fledging business added little to our monthly income. Right now, she was right, but I knew in time, she'd be a huge success.

When I hopped into the living room trying to juggle putting on shoes and walking, I saw the same news story about that Forner bitch broadcasting again. *Police forensics are scouring her apartment.* "Turn that off. You don't need to be listening to that all day." I swallowed hard and regretted the statement.

Angel stood by the counter with something wrapped in a napkin getting smaller as she began to compress the contents in a closing fist. "I like to watch the morning news."

"Just turn it off, please." The "please" was an afterthought, because I know my tone had made a drastic change from five minutes earlier.

"And here I thought the stick up your ass was gone." She grabbed the remote from the kitchen counter and silenced the broadcast, but the one in my head played on.

Once my shoe settled on my foot, I headed to the door.

"Don't you want this?" She opened her fist with the crumpled breakfast sandwich resting in her hand like she'd crushed it on the sidewalk.

"I'm not hungry." I reached for the doorknob.

"Jordan?" When I turned, I expected to see an

angry wife, but instead I saw confusion and concern.

"I hope your day gets better," she said.

"So do I." An icy chill spread through my body as I stepped into the hall of the building. I leaned my back against the wall. Complete silence filled the space, but one thought pierced my brain. My hand brushed my forearm.

Chances are high they'll find my DNA.

Chapter Three
Angel

Something was wrong.

I was the one who had perfected the angry outbursts. I mean Jordan got mad on occasion, but usually because of something stupid I did. Even at that, today this was different. He was different.

He wasn't angry at me.

This was internal.

In some ways, I believed as Jordan did. Jessica out of the picture solved our problem. I wanted the problem gone, but celebrating our freedom from this clusterfuck seemed to invite bad karma.

We had no way of knowing how people would react if they found out. Chances are my dad would not be reading any story Jessica wrote. If the story wasn't about sports or an obituary, my dad didn't read it.

So Dad was out, but still once one person we knew read the reveal, then the dominoes would keep falling until our vibrant, pretty world imploded. Indianapolis was a big city, but not so big we wouldn't be recognized and ostracized for expressing our love a little left of center. Okay, more left than most, but still. It's not like we'd killed anyone.

****

I don't know whether the manuscript I was editing was amazing, engaging, or I was worried about Jordan, but whatever the case, the ding from my phone gave me such a start, I had to grab the sides of the chair to keep from falling Once I realized I wasn't in the midst of a heart attack, I checked who was texting me.

—*Would you open the door?*—

Shit. I'd forgotten about Bri coming over.

—*Why didn't you knock?*—

—*I did 4 or 5 times.*—

I raced to open the door, only to see her sitting on the floor against the wall. "Oh, it hasn't been *that* long."

When she glanced in my direction, her face flushed.

"Oh, I know that look. Get a text from Cameron?"

She squirmed and narrowed her eyes, but made no attempt to stand.

I reached and swiped the phone from her hand.

She screamed and like a tiger on a deer sprang from the floor. "Give me that."

I read the screen getting a little aroused myself. "Damn, girl. Why are you even here?"

She snatched her phone back and stuffed it in her purse. "I can't exactly go to his office."

"I bet there's a lock on the door."

"Stop it." Cherry. I believe her face resembled a cherry now.

She followed me into the condo and to my kitchen. I poured her a mug of the shit Jordan called coffee—which he didn't even drink this morning.

"You know, as long as I've known you, minus the recent and resolved separation, never in my most fucked up notions did I picture you and Cameron as a couple."

She shrugged and sipped the crude oil in a cup. "Jordan's coffee is getting better."

"You two." The eye roll was the most exercise I'd had all morning.

"I suppose you heard the news this morning." Without breaking her eye contact, Bri slipped onto the barstool. I recognized her stare penetrating into my inner thoughts trying to extract without mercy any secrets I harbored.

"I heard it. You know as much as I do, though. By the way, nice deflection from you and Cameron."

"Not a deflection. I just wondered. What did Jordan say?"

A mimosa sounded good this morning, but we only had the orange juice part of the concoction so I poured myself a tall glass of juice and plopped myself on the counter. "Nice, second deflection that I'll get back to, but Jordan was really weird this morning when he heard. He wasn't himself at all."

Bri closed her eyes taking a long and slow sip as if savoring the moment she tasted the best coffee on the planet. Not so long ago, she thought his coffee sucked. Boy, everything had changed with her. My husband would be thrilled about the coffee. He wasn't the least bit thrilled about Bri's other big life change. I shook my head.

"What do you mean he wasn't himself? How did he act?"

As soon as I drew my knees to my chest and my bare feet touched the counter, I lost my train of thought. Cold granite sent shivers through my legs, but before the chill crested my knees, another kind of heat invaded reminding me of the last time we used this space. "I'm sorry what did you say?"

"Where did you go, girl? I asked how did Jordan act."

So slick and smooth. I lightly brushed my fingers across the rock. "We've had lots of great times on this counter."

Bri shoved away from the counter so fast, she backpedaled to keep from falling, while her coffee mug thudded against granite from her quick release. "Eww. Did you have to tell me that?"

She flapped her hands in the air as if the motion would release the sex residue. Not that there was any…I didn't think there was, but who knows.

"Calm down. We clean up after ourselves. You know, bring out the firehose and disinfectant. Gets a little slippery sometimes with sweat and…"

"Stop."

Wow. She covered her ears.

"Are you sure you and Cameron…?" I had to laugh at the daggers flying from her eyes.

"Can we get back to the original conversation?" Bri returned to the stool, but kept her hands in her lap.

"What was the original conversation?" The granite memories lingered, and I'm sure were better than what we were talking about.

She shook her head. "Your husband. We were talking about Jordan acting strange."

I slumped. "Oh yeah, that. I was fixing breakfast and I heard the newscaster say Jessica's name and what happened. I yelled for him to come watch, and when he did…It was weird. His response was more of relief than shock. Granted I kinda hated her, but I wasn't happy she's dead."

Now the counter did chill my body, but not even the previous memories gave me any warmth. "I called him on it, and he was sorry. Got happy again and said we'd have a session tonight, but when he saw the TV still on, and they were repeating the story, he got all pissed again and left."

"That's a little weird I'd say." Downing the rest of her coffee she said, "You know, I saw her a few days ago."

"Really. Where?"

"Umm, at Koffees." She wiggled on the stool almost slipping over the back.

Because my casual position on my counter seemed to bother Bri, I slid to the floor. Glancing at the clock on the microwave, I considered making a rum run. I needed something stronger than the juice and mixing rum, coke, and lime seemed like a good idea. However, one usually led to two or three, and at times four. I still worked under the assumption my husband and I had some bondage business on the planner. If my husband detected an appearance of a buzz or my body language hinted I'd been buzzed at some point in the day, Jordan would nix the whole thing and I would get to hear a lecture about responsible kink.

These weeknight locked sessions were precursors to the more extended ones we saved for weekends. The more and longer these sessions became, the more I craved them. Hot sex notwithstanding, I loved the challenges. Not the challenge of holding an orgasm—still failing. Not the challenge of tight bonds—fucking loved that. Not the challenge of pleasing my husband. At the risk of sounding cocky, I rock that. No, for me the biggest challenge was sound.

Jordan loved quiet.

I hated it.

Once he told me he'd give me five hundred dollars to buy shoes if I kept from talking for a twenty-four hour session. I lasted two and a half hours—personal best. He made the bet because he knew there was no way in hell he'd lose a dime.

I think I have adult ADD. "You saw her? Was she with anyone? That might be a clue. Although Jordan was adamant about not going to the police telling them what she was doing."

Bri's wiggling bumped up a few notches.

"What is wrong with you? Is something trying to crawl up your ass?"

"Nothing is wrong. I really can't say if she was with someone. The place was really crowded."

"That's too bad. Maybe the police will find something in her apartment."

Chapter Four
Jordan

"Jordan."

Mr. Levendar's voice interrupted my thoughts with such a blast, my hand flinched, and I tipped my coffee mug but recovered without spilling any in my lap. Even though we were a smaller subsidiary of his larger corporation, Bernhard Levendar always respectcd the boundaries of an office. He leaned his head inside the open doorway.

"Mr. Levendar. I apologize. I was going over some things in my head." I stood in response. "Come in."

The regal old man smiled. "It must have been something grand. I stood there a bit before I even called your name. I hope it's a moneymaker for us." He entered my office and the leather chair opposite my desk squeaked as he sat. "I wanted to talk to you about some of our clients."

Knowing the gist of this conversation, I went to shut my office door before sitting down. "Sure. Has anyone complained?"

Oh no," he said vigorously shaking his head. "Quite the contrary. Marlon Straymeyer couldn't stop singing the praises of his evening." He leaned closer. "Jordan, I know this isn't exactly written in your job description, but I do appreciate what you do. And you do it so well. You have a bigger future here."

I wasn't as thrilled with his compliment as maybe I should have been. Mr. Levendar had been good to me. He hired me knowing my fuck up at my previous job, and I worked hard to convince everyone here above me I could be the best employee. When I earned the marketing manager job, I wasn't still naïve enough to believe the conference room multi-media presentations were what wowed and wooed certain clients. Some of our clients disgusted me, but they had the business we wanted so they had us by the balls.

"I understand it's part of the job, but I really don't like lying to my wife."

At the mention of Angel, Mr. Levendar smiled deeply. The first time she met him, she charmed him as quickly as she did me.

"I get that, but I'm sure if she knew, Emma would realize it's about business. She's a very smart woman and sweet as can be."

He'd never seen her angry.

"Cameron has filled in for you a few times. I'll ask him to fill in a little more often until he leaves. He's not attached, so he shouldn't have a problem. However, that's a very short term solution."

"Yeah, well…" I picked up a pen and began tapping on my desk. That fucker was infringing even more in my life. "He's attached now."

Noticing my less than joyful attitude, he raised an inquisitive eyebrow. "I know you two don't care for each other, but you do work well together. So, why does his having a girlfriend disrupt anything?"

"I don't see it disrupting anything in the office. His new girlfriend is Emma's best friend. He's leaving for Chicago soon, but we'll still be connected."

At that, he roared with laughter. Yeah, pretty fucking funny.

"You know, Jordan, it's the little things that bite us in the ass that hurt the most." He slapped his hands on his legs as he stood. "I'll stop by Cameron's office and ask him to help out a little more until he leaves."

"Thank you. I'm surprising Emma with a long weekend getaway, and that's one less thing to worry about." *And one less thing for her to find out about*.

After he left, I still couldn't relax. I kept waiting for a cop to walk through my door.

"Caldera. Levendar said you wanted to see me." Unlike Mr. Levendar, Terry strolled into my office like he paid the mortgage.

Fuck.

Better than a cop but still...

"I didn't ask to talk to you. He said he'd talk to you about taking a few of special clients this week."

He grinned. "Is there some sort of dirty ole man convention in town?"

He was joking, but sometimes I wondered. I raked my hands through my hair wishing they were Angel's instead of mine. My head tingled remembering how she scraped her nails across my scalp. Tiny electrical pulses zipped from the roots of my hair pumping my dick even more than I thought possible. "I don't know why the hell they want to be here now. I had three last week and four this week. It's getting ridiculous all piling on at once."

My eyes narrowed and my temperature boiled when he casually flopped a hip down on my desk.

"I can take tonight, but not Friday. I booked the private balcony at the Boatyard for dinner for Sabrina and me."

"Special occasion?"

Chatty Terry went radio silent. A sick feeling began creeping into my stomach. "Fuck me. Please, for the love of God no."

If I fisted that smug smile off his mouth, I wondered if I'd get fired. He was leaving the company anyway.

"Just think of the couples' weekends, trips up north for the Taste of Chicago. Maybe I'll find a playgroup for all of us when you visit. Christmas, New Years, Memorial Day weekend. This'll be fun."

He winked. He fucking winked at me. "You wouldn't keep Emma from her best friend would you?"

"When's your last day?"

"Couple weeks."

"Then get the fuck out of my office. If you need to talk to me…send me an email." For one of the few times in my life, I believed alcohol was the answer to this day.

He laughed as he stood. "Man, you're too easy. Although, I can see what Emma sees in you. You're hot when you're hot."

With the same confident ease he strolled in with, he strolled out until he reached the threshold of my office. When he turned, I saw his expression go from teasing to solemn. "I heard your little problem went away. I guess things will be better for you both."

"Yeah."

For now.

Chapter Five
Angel

A kaleidoscope of color flashed on the balcony wall. Sunlight beamed and projected through the prism of diamonds on my wedding ring and danced along the brick with each animated wave of my hand.

Sabrina left over an hour ago, and I had accomplished nothing but a child's game of shadow dancing with my ring.

During our visit, her emotions entered and exited a revolving door of happy, confused, scared, and thrilled. She loved Cameron, but was their relationship happening too fast? I wasn't the best judge of that since I'm the one who sorta begged Jordan to have sex with me after a few dates. Her discovery of a new sexual identity confused her. I could relate, and like me, she was afraid someone would find out—namely her parents. I really didn't see that happening. Who talked about sex with their parents? And Cameron thrilled, confused, and scared the beejeezus out of her with every touch and command.

"Allow yourself to be happy because you're happy and don't question the method," I told her. Every day I woke up with hot breath warming the thin cord of leather on the collar I wore and his wooden pole stuck in my back. My happiness.

My home filled with the scents of love. That God-awful to me coffee smell hung in the kitchen like a fleece blanket. Although months had passed since the last s'mores and wine in front of the fireplace, hints of wood and smoke tickled my nose. Anytime I needed a boost, I rolled myself in the sheets from our bed filled with the smells of being human—sex and sweat with mixes of the sea, citrus, jasmine, and the occasional smear of chocolate.

While our second bedroom often served as our playroom, the pleasure tools rested out of sight in a dresser sitting in the closet. Some days under the guise of cleaning, I went to the dresser and pulled out a drawer. As the contents revealed themselves to me, I still heard a slight gasp escaping my lips. The scent of leather enticed my fingers to caress the supple smoothness of the cuffs and the soft padding lining them. The flogger and crop sat side by side. One day I hoped Jordan would be the one slapping my skin and not the mystery master.

Even though the sight and scents of the toys made me horny, at least half of the time I refrained from pleasuring myself. Jordan could always tell and then he'd make me do it again while he watched. It was my punishment because I couldn't fight off an orgasm like my husband could. So many times when he held the candle dripping over me...good God I lost any remnant of the control I struggled to grasp. I wondered if our den of pleasure would ever serve any other purpose.

Even with the distractions I managed to create, my mind found moments throughout the day to think about Jessica Forner. Paired with thinking about her death, guilt lodged in my belly, hammering nails in my stomach and sawed away at my belief I was indeed a good person.

I know at some point throughout this whole disaster of trying to remain anonymous, I'm sure I likely said, either I wished her dead or that I wanted to kill her. Neither were true, but now knowing the reason our secret would remain safe made me believe somehow I was an accessory to her death. Not only that, Jordan's attitude about the whole thing perplexed me.

Jordan was one of the all-around nicest persons I'd ever met. Other than Cameron, he played well with others. Even at that, his confrontations with Cameron amounted to verbal chest bumping and dick measuring. I doubted Jordan had ever been in a physical fight in his life.

Maybe I over-analyzed the whole thing. He'd not been in the best of moods the last couple of weeks. Work had not ended at five o'clock, but dragged on for hours later entertaining clients. Apparently, even dining at the best restaurants got old after a while. Sometimes he asked me to go because on occasion male clients brought their wives or girlfriends along. When I found out a few clients had both wives and girlfriends, I told Jordan I wanted no part of that meal and he shouldn't either. He said he didn't condone their actions, but he preferred to remain employed.

Not once in the last two weeks had I attended any dinners.

Once I finished with light sabering the wall with my ring, I'd planned to open my laptop and work. The squirrel in my plan had me deconstructing the pedestrians walking along the canal. From my upper level vantage point, I dismantled and sorted their professions, marital statuses, reasons for being on the canal walk, and clothing. No reason or excuse exists to wear those rubber shoes in public. If you cannot descend steps in five-inch heels without looking like a baby giraffe trying to stand, don't wear them.

An incoming text interrupted my running commentary.

—*On my way home. Couple stops to make.*—

My reply. —*You want me to start dinner?*—

—*No. I'll take care of it.*—

Turned out to be good news for me. I never had any real intention of cooking dinner. I'd have flipped through the pile of takeout menus and called for delivery.

With a disinclined sigh I abandoned my cherished spot on the balcony to make the necessary wardrobe change from nerd slob to woman ready to be fucked with delicious and merciless abandon. I hoped one, Jordan hadn't changed his mind, and two, he'd resolved whatever was up his ass this morning.

I didn't quite see how my mass of curls left to its own decision making made his dick hard, but I allowed them the freedom to dry naturally. In my opinion, I thought I looked like an explosion of clown-car occupants. As I was slipping on my robe, I heard his key in the door and I cut a confident path to the living room in the five-inch black stilettos I could rock like a professional escort. If this editing thing didn't work out, maybe the high-paid hooker profession would.

As soon as I saw his reaction, my concerns dissipated into the already heated air between us. He carried two paper shopping bags. One contained two bouquets of roses and the other I had no clue.

"You hardly ever bring me flowers."

Setting both bags on the counter, he turned to close the gap in three steps. "I know, and I should more often. This time…"

His large hand settled against my neck and his thumb stroked from my jaw to my collar. With each swipe, hazy clouds twirled in front of my eyes and a string of misty charge traveled down my spine.

"They aren't for you either. I mean, you can't put them in a vase." Both of his hands grasped the sides of my neck and his thumbs gently forced my jaw upward. I swallowed hard.

I knew everything about this man. I knew every ridge on his thumbs and counted until all three rippled across my skin. I knew even after all day long, he still smelled of sun, ocean, and citrus. I knew his eyes changed from light to dark and burned through me like a laser. I flushed knowing exactly how his tongue made me primal.

I knew everything about this man, and that's why I shivered.

Trying to gain a little control, I backed away from his hold and moved to the bag not containing roses. "What's for dinner?"

A sudden yank on my hair stopped me. "Not so fast, Angel."

"Jordan, I'm hungry. I didn't eat lunch."

"Why not?"

"Because I thought you'd bring something really awesome home for dinner." I held my ground and so did he. My hair became a tightrope between us.

"I didn't text you until late today. Why would you think I was bringing dinner?" Hand over hand across my hair, he stepped and pulled until we met in the center.

He should know by now the kind of explanation he'd receive. "Well, I figured you'd call and ask what we were having for dinner. Then I'd say 'Oops, I forgot to take anything out of the freezer. I guess bacon and eggs.' Then you'd say 'never mind. I'll pick something up on the way home.'" Cheshire cat smile and growling stomach. "So, it all worked out. What're we having?"

Ouch. One hand tightened his grip on the roots of my hair. I never should have yanked his hair in the car when we left the party that time. I get periodic reminders that it's not pleasant until you're about to orgasm.

Raised eyebrow meant chastisement would commence. "You do know the clock has started on our play session?"

I was ravenous and decided asking for forgiveness later was my plan of action. "It smells killer. Where did you go?"

I heard something like a sigh mixed with a growl, and tally one for me the winner of round one.

"Do you do this on purpose or you really can't help yourself?"

"Do what?" I flashed a coy smile.

"Ig. Nore. Me."

I batted my eyelashes. "No, Sir. I don't ignore you, but if I don't eat soon, I may be too weak to participate later. And you wouldn't want that…would you?"

He bit my ear, released my hair, and said, "Stay out of the bag until I go change, you master manipulator."

Internal fist pump.

Chapter Six
Jordan

As I changed into jeans, I wondered how many days would pass before the cops discovered we had a connection to Jessica. Those thoughts occupied my head the whole day. Nausea burned in my stomach all day and like Angel, I hadn't eaten either.

Even though I'd planned our evening before I heard the news, I needed tonight more than anything. In the fleeting moments of sanctuary, my Angel would clear my mind of the difficulty we might soon face.

Angel makes the most glorious sounds, and the more she's restricted, the more her songs dance in my ears and control my body. She's fire. She's burned her essence into my soul, and I can't survive without her music.

A lottery ticket fell from my jacket pocket. Most people make plans for expensive cars, big homes, or mega vacations. I'd planned to quit my job and spend day and night with my dick inside her.

I went to the other bedroom to prepare a few things for our evening. I knew Angel would enjoy this one. She loved nostalgia.

"Jordan, dammit, hurry up. If you don't get in here soon, I'm goin' to eat without you. This smell is killing me."

"You do, and you'll be sorry." I didn't know how,

but I'd think of something.

"You're all talk."

Damn her. She pushed everything to the edge. I *was* all talk. Every kind of punishment I'd ever tried backfired. She liked it. No, she didn't like it; she fuckin' loved it. She glistened like morning dew from every decision I made.

She needed her ass cherry red.

We'll see.

I stuffed a few pieces of wrapped chocolate in my pocket warming until the foil relaxed under the softening square I'd use later. In the kitchen, I caught her pulling the containers from the bag. "This looks and smells like heaven, like Ernie's."

"It is from Ernie's."

She narrowed her eyes and lifted the plastic lid from the foil box. "Since when does Ernie's Steak House do carry out?"

Every now and then, I called in a favor. "Since Mackinzie Branham became the head chef."

She set the container of ribeye steak, red-skinned mashed potatoes, and creamed spinach on the counter and retrieved the other one as well. "Mackinzie Branham."

I swear I could see the inner works of her brain performing an SEO for results. For all her silliness and sexiness, most of the time Angel was the smartest person in the room.

"Is he that guy who comes to the parties and sits and watches? He's hot as all get out, but kind of creepy. He's never talked to me."

"Not supposed to talk to you." Interesting how women rate men on their hotness and men rate them on whether or not we could kick their ass.

"So how does he rank on the 'I could probably kick his ass' meter?"

A smile tugged at my face. We knew each other pretty well…for the most part. "I'm taller than he is, but he's good with knives. So, I think I'll let that one go."

The whole time she dished out food onto plates, every movement fluttered the short silky red robe exposing her long lean legs. As I scanned from her lacy underwear to the stilettos, my jeans began to crush my crotch. Fuck, could she walk a shoe. Not once had I ever bitched about the cost of her shoes. The rate of return for my cock far outweighed the clutter in the closet.

The scent of seasoned steak tickled my nose. Sure I was ravenous, but not for steak.

Angel strutted to the dining room table with plates in hand and ass wiggling with every step. That line about women not knowing how they affect men, at least in Angel's case, is complete bullshit. She choreographed each step for maximum boner effect.

"Are you coming?" She glanced over her shoulder—her bare leg jutting out from beneath the robe.

Soon. Very soon.

"So, tell me about this Mackinzie guy. The odds of me ever being able to speak with him are slim." She pointed her fork at me while she chewed.

"I don't know. He's kinda new in town, just got divorced."

"Is he a Dom or a voyeur?" Angel pushed away her plate with most of the food still untouched.

"Is something wrong with your food?"

She propped an elbow on the table and rested her chin in her hand. Subtlety not being her strong suit, Angel's eyes rested on my hands. I know she was wondering what my hands would do to her later.

A flush of crimson spread across her face. "It's fine. I don't want to get too full for later. Now, is Mackinzie a Dominant?"

"Yes, he is. He's getting the lay of the land." I set my fork on the table. "I don't really care about Mack right now. If you're finished, go do what you need to do and be back here in ten minutes." Ten minutes was way too long. "Don't make me wait."

****

Other than lipstick and maybe a little mascara, Angel returned with little change. Well, she had loosened the belt on the robe and instead of black lace edges of a bra I expected, I saw nothing, as in firm, smooth, and creamy breasts I would later brand red with my teeth. She still wore the underwear, but we'd remedy that very soon.

I stood and reached my hand to hers. Her hands seemed so tiny in mine—a dime in a well. Warm and soft, but her pulse pounded and radiated through me.

Intertwining my hand with hers, I wrapped my other arm around her waist underneath the robe. While her hand was warm, her body sizzled, and her satiny skin breezed across my palm with the lightness of a feather.

"I love you." I nuzzled her neck, and her curls shrouded my head in ringlets of silk. I inhaled deeply taking in the flowery scent she wore. The very first time we met, that same scent captivated me as we danced and lured me into a web I refused to escape. Every morning before I even opened my eyes, Angel's scent gave me life. "You've given me the greatest gifts—more than I ever deserved."

I raked my teeth across her neck, scraping the ridge of the collar. She moaned softly and tilted her head to expose more flesh. I scraped again, and then I bit…hard and sucked her skin between my teeth. A throaty gasp turned into a louder moan—the sound of her arousal fueled my own desire. I bit and sucked again and again, knowing my work on her canvas would greet me in the morning with vivid color.

"You're mine, Angel."

She responded with pushing her body hard against the front of my jeans. "Yes."

"Tell me."

"I'm yours, Sir."

"Tell me again."

"All yours. Always yours, forever."

She couldn't take a breath before I crushed her lips to mine and invaded with my tongue…claiming, commanding. In this, Angel always yielded to me. But not shrinking. No, she invited and then accepted my vicious exploration inside.

I felt her hands on the zipper of my jeans. In my intoxication, she'd managed to slip her hand from mine. I had to stop this or we'd never get to my original plan. "Ah-ah-ah." I grabbed her wrists. "We have work to do."

Chapter Seven
Angel

I stumbled.

I stumbled because Jordan had sucked from my body the ability to follow simple commands from my brain…like walking. I knew what the night was supposed to be, but his little act of foreplay had so much pressure built up in my prurient chamber I was about to blow a gasket.

Although I didn't quite understand his whispered mandate, I'd responded. Of course I was his—not chattel, but our spirits were one, and our physical connection blew my mind. In the same token, he belonged to me. Once, after a fight, I told him his dick still belonged to me and not to even think about being stingy because he was pissed. My ownership ran pretty deep.

Once in the room, I scanned the area looking for clues of my impending climax. Red silk rope lay coiled on the bed. A blindfold rested on a small box.

The box.

Fuck me.

The box contained nipple clamps. I could deal with and in a hard to explain way, enjoyed the in between part, but putting on hurt like a son of a bitch and removing were a holy hell of fire. The only other thing I saw was the chair we rarely used anymore.

A tickle spread from the back of my neck to my shoulders when Jordan slowly began to slip the robe from me. Somewhere between point A and point B, Jordan had removed his shirt, and the exchange of heat passing between us became a branding iron of radiance.

I turned my head slightly waiting for instruction.

He ran his knuckles across my cheek. "I thought a little Throwback Thursday."

Ah, I get it now. The chair.

"But what about the nip…"

"Well." He wrapped his arms around my shoulders and rested his chin on top of my head. "Maybe more of a reboot Thursday."

"Oh."

"Do you know what you look like when you wear those?"

"Like I'm about ready to pass out?"

His whole body vibrated into mine with his chuckle.

"You look like the queen who rules over my every fantasy."

A rather lofty honor. "I wish there was a way to jump to the middle without having to go through the initial vising and the subsequent sensation of the fires of Hell."

"Don't you worry. I'll distract you." He released his hold. "Now go sit and take off the panties first."

My hand went to my thigh, circling the tiny scar— my enduring *tattoo* of my first time. I hooked my thumbs in the waist of my underwear and slipped them over my hips never breaking eye contact with my husband. As his breathing increased and he clenched his jaw, his cock hardened beneath the heavy denim.

"Angel, if you don't hurry up, I'll cut them again."

I wasn't too slow.

I was too much.

He failed to hide how I affected him.

Make no mistake. If the situation were reversed, I'd fare no better.

After my panties hit the floor, I lifted my foot to my ass to pull off my shoe. "No, no, no. Leave them on." His clipped and low tone sounded dangerous and full of sin.

"If you're going to wear FMPs, you're gonna wear them while you're getting fucked. I may use them for a handle, or maybe I'll use the heel as a rope anchor."

He pushed me forward to the chair. "Sit. Now."

Reminiscent of the first time, butterflies swirled in my stomach. The difference…my screams would have nothing to do with fear.

I barely settled myself on the chair when complete darkness consumed my vision. *The curtain comes down, and the show begins.*

"It's always better when you don't know what's coming." A wicked whisper spiraled into my ear so inflaming, the uncomfortable ache returned, and I had to shift my weight to quell the mounting arousal.

Ouch. One day his teeth were going to put a hole in my ear big enough for one of those pie pans.

"Spread your wings, Angel."

The scrape of my heels against the wood floor amplified by my darkness, rattled my ears and sent reverberating tingles down my spine. Jordan's strong but gentle touch aligned my feet to the chair legs and he bound each ankle with the rope. Next, he wrapped my knees higher and tighter on the chair, and I was completely exposed with no possible way to cover my goods.

So I waited.

A warm sensation brushed my ankle previewing the brief feather-soft kiss whispered against my skin.

Each kiss moved higher, became hotter, and challenged my body to fight the tingling exploding against the millions of my nerve endings and taking a hammer to anything close to my pussy.

I became so absorbed in his sweet torture, I had forgotten my hands and arms were free. Seizing the opportunity before he realized, I leaned forward to lose my fingers deep in the strands of hair hanging over his forehead.

He moaned when I scraped my nails across his scalp. This wasn't at all like the first time.

"Jordan," I managed to utter because another surge of pleasure pulsed.

"Mmm, what, Angel?"

Wow, I was talking and not being chastised. "I thought this was throwback Thursday."

He stopped short of the threshold of my pleasure palace. "I said reboot."

Well okay, then.

Once Jordan arrived to my thigh, inner thigh to be exact, I clenched. I knew he would sink his teeth into me again and again.

Fuck, that hurts. Do it again.

Fuck, that hurts. Keep doing it.

Ever since Jordan magnified the biting thing, I had to admit I was a little embarrassed I was insatiable. I'd see the purple marks on my legs and smile—reminders of him. The only problem was that I had to be careful about wearing skirts when dotted with love. He seemed to like my marks on him too. I'd never heard a complaint other than "don't bite the neck again." Pretty sure it had to do with meeting million dollar clients sporting a major league hickey.

He'd arrived.

He kissed and nipped all around my opening, and I alternated between a hot bubble bath of bliss and the sting of stepping on a thumbtack.

I slid my hands from his hair to the back of his neck—his corded muscles taut and fiery beneath my fingers. This free rein of touching made me even hotter. Jordan's brand of torture made me until after I'd orgasmed to start my exploration of his body. Confused or not, I took every advantage he allowed me now.

Jordan cupped my ass cheeks with his hands and moved me a little closer to where I teetered on the brink of falling off the chair. With his head between my legs, the heat from his head seared my thighs and tiny strands of hair tickled my delicate skin. Even though I knew the next step, I flinched as his sweet tongue knocked on my door before barging in seconds later.

Holy shit. I'll never get tired of this.

Each lick, lap, swish, and nip was a hot ocean wave of *Dayyumm,* and the tide kept coming faster and more intense.

Shit.

As expected, he stopped, pushed my ass flush against the back of the chair and removed his presence from me.

"Jordan," I whined. "You do know that when you do that, it's physically painful for me?"

"I do." The husky, gritty voice of a man also in

need broke through the darkness.

A sudden rush of air swept by and then a heavy weight landed in my lap. Jordan sat on me. I know he faced me because no sooner had I adjusted to the weight than his lips crushed mine, clanging our teeth together. When he pushed his tongue inside, I tasted myself—not a bad taste but not something that will ever be a soda or ice cream flavor. It's weird.

I seized my opportunity again and squeezed my arms around his neck harder until he moaned with his own pleasure. His hands imprisoned my face as he continued his frenzied attack on my lips.

I accepted it. Not because I had to, which I sorta did, but because I needed to.

I needed so much more. If I had the ability to crawl inside of him and stay forever, I would.

Any other time his weight crushed me, but the adrenaline pumping through my body from his touch gave me superhero shields of strength.

His hands eased their hold, and he pulled away from the kiss. I felt Jordan's arms reach around behind me. "I want you to hold on to the chair seat…or do I need to bind your wrists?"

That was a loaded question. Either way whatever was coming required a lot of self-control—something I generally lacked. "I can do it," I said with wavering conviction.

Our connection was so strong, I sensed him smile. The ever so slight shift in his weight—I perceived as a smile.

Jordan began chewing on my shoulder. The sensation always zapped its way down to my ass, and I squirmed. He kept the waves of tingles in motion, and I still gripped the chair. I could do this, no prob…

Fuck!

The bite of the clamp getting a chokehold on my nipple almost ripped my fingers out of place. Even worse, I knew I had one more nipple, and I almost thought the anticipation was worse than…

Shit.

Nope, No, it wasn't.

"Breathe, Angel."

By the third deep breath, the vise had lessened to a pinch and then the delicious taunting began. An itch, an ache, a something twirled in my boobs, and I opened my eyes wide behind the blindfold, and when he tugged on the chain, I squeezed the chair so hard, I no longer had feeling in my fingers. I began to think I'd unseated my husband when I bucked. "Oh, Jordan. I, I…"

"You like me yanking your chain?"

He licked my nipple and a thousand volts of sizzle arced across the chain. With his weight on my lap I could do nothing but imaginary stomps of my feet and cry out until my throat ached. Our walls weren't so thick that if I were to see Mr. Walker in the hall, I'd turn red and he'd smile.

"Maybe, we should have used the gag," he whispered. "But you know what? Every sound you make gets me harder and harder until I hurt."

He was right. That bulge in his jeans pressed like an iron rod against my belly.

His teeth clanged across the chain—pulling as they traveled to the other end. I tried to resist moving forward with the chain, but the euphoria ignited from the light tugs shifted to teeth gritting stabs of pain.

Jordan's rhythmic massage of my breasts sending

more blood to the dam already threatening to burst. I swear I saw millions of tiny stars dancing in front of my covered face. When he reached my other nipple, the tiny little tweak with his teeth sent a rush signal shooting to my happy place. I squirmed beneath his legs trying to raise my hips. I couldn't hold out much longer. My arousal surged with such power I was ready to go at any second.

How did that happen?

How do you climax with nothing inside your walls?

Jordan must have sensed my readiness. "Don't you dare. Don't you dare."

"I'm trying." The words seethed through my breathless body.

"Try harder."

"Bastard."

He chuckled and leaped from my lap. Then nothing.

Complete silence filled my head, and the spinning top of my throbbing parts slowed.

Damn him.

I still gripped the edges of the chair. I didn't want to ruin the possibility of using my hands later by disobeying now.

The silence and the darkness slowed the time in my head. A cave of vulnerability swallowed me.

Chapter Eight
Jordan

She fought her own body for control.

I stood in the doorway watching her. If I moved any closer, she'd detect my presence. She had a nose like a Bloodhound.

Her chest heaved in a rhythmic ballet with her head rising and lowering with every breath. That wild mass of hair seemed to spring from her head like a Medusa. Blindfolded and bound to the chair and with her hands gripping the chair seat, yes, she appeared vulnerable waiting for me to devour her.

No, my Angel wasn't vulnerable. She was a Siren who lured me from the boat to drown in the depths of her soul. She gladly accepted what I gave her and wanted more than I gave. She fought me and challenged me. She surprised and seduced me every day. If anything, she preyed on me replacing my blood with hers.

My Angel—the devil herself and sexy as sin.

Even though my bare feet didn't make a sound I thought, before I reached the dresser in the closet, I saw her head snap my direction. "Sir?"

Nose like a damn Bloodhound. "What it is, baby?"

"Just making sure you hadn't left me."

My bare back chilled as I opened the drawer containing what I wanted. "I'll never leave you."

I grabbed what I was looking for, and set one item on the top of the dresser while I switched on the phone I kept in the drawer. I used this for taking pictures of my wife bound with exquisite beauty. If we stayed in a session during the week, I sometimes took the phone with me and sent her dirty texts or instructions. She hated when I denied her underwear, and that's why I did it. Frustrated and annoyed Angel was even hotter. I exchanged the phone for the other object and approached her.

When I knelt between her legs, I caressed her inner thigh with my hand. Her muscles contracted. "A little tense are we?"

"I'm more than ready for you to take off these clamps."

"Hurts when I do it, doesn't it?"

"Like a mother fucker."

"My dear, you never disappoint."

I pressed the button on the vibrator to the rapid pulse setting, and the device filled the room with its buzzing.

"Shit," came a whisper in the dark. "Jordan?"

"You know Mr. Walker will be grateful. Your voice is amazing." I wasn't the only one who got a woody from Angel's vocal talents. On more than one occasion when we passed in the hall, I swear our neighbor wanted to high five me. The man was an eighty-five year old retired obstetrician. I think he kept waiting for a formal announcement of a baby on the way. Not right now.

The smooth and tender skin on her thigh warmed my hand with hot pulses. She trembled with the same cadence of the tool of her impending upheaval.

I couldn't resist one more taste before hitting her with the juice. I swept my tongue around the outside of her sweet spot, and she giggled. I know her so well. This wasn't a giggle because my tongue tickled.

The waiting made her nervous. Angel had no patience and waiting was the playground for her nerves. I decided to end her agony, because I was anxious to get on with the second round of my plan.

Little by little, I inserted the vibrator until squeaky moans filled the air. I went deeper and upped the intensity. Angel's cries amped up as well. She writhed under the stimulation, but still managed to hold onto the chair.

"I can't. I can't. God, please stop." She was such a liar. If I stopped, she'd chew my ear off with disgruntled elocution. That's why our new agreement included safewords.

"You want to come don't you?"

"Yes."

I pulled out the vibrator.

"You're a son of a bitch. You know that?"

I loved our exchanges. I don't know what I'd do if I lost them. "Such language. Filthy-mouthed girls don't deserve rewards."

"Yes they do." She panted. "This filthy mouth can do some pretty damn good stuff."

Yes it can.

I pushed the control to the max setting and plunged it deep inside her, working everywhere until her writhing legs began to weaken the bonds. I could make out the trickle of perspiration sliding down the side of her face and following the curve of her jaw before dropping onto her chest.

The metal chain between her nipples sang from the bouncing. She danced from the torment, and I knew I had to end this or I was a goner as well. "Let it go, Angel. I love to hear your orgasm."

At the peak of her release, I reached to release the clamps, and she screamed even louder from the blood rush. She collapsed against the chair with her arms dangling from her side.

I rushed to undo the ropes and slumped to the floor with her in my lap. She buried her face into my shoulder—her body still trembling and short on breath. Sticky skin and sweaty hair filled my heart.

"Your throat a little sore?"

"Yes," came a hoarse reply.

I hugged her tighter. "I'm surprised you can talk at all. I'll get you some water. Rest a bit so we can continue."

She went stiff. "Continue?"

I discarded the blindfold, wrapped her hair around my fist and pulled her head to face me. "Oh, baby, I told you we were going all night."

Chapter Nine
Angel

I had no legs.

Somewhere in the middle of all that my legs melted or exploded into some nether world. I had no sense I even had lower extremities. It's a very odd feeling. Like if Jordan picked me up, he'd only be holding a torso. I raised my head to peer down my body. Legs were there, but I, when I came, I must have released Novocain.

Jordan's bulge dug into my hip so I fumbled around to find the zipper on his jeans. My legs may not work, but I still had hands. Unfortunately, so did he, and he stopped me from invading him.

"Not yet." He brought my hand to his lips placing soft and tingling kisses to my palm. His tongue followed the lines on my hand, and the tender skin between my thumb and forefinger throbbed. Exhausted, but I was already climbing again on the climax elevator.

"Can you get up?"

I nodded and pushed myself from his lap. While Jordan stood, I couldn't tear my eyes away from his magnificent presence. His Italian ancestry showed with his olive skin and deep brown hair. I'm not sure where the blue eyes came from, but when they penetrated mine, I went weak in the knees. And his stare in no uncertain words told me my body was about to be consumed. Is it weird to drool over your own husband?

I stood on wobbly legs for a few seconds before he picked me up and carried me to the kitchen. He sat me on the island which now looked more like an altar than a counter. He'd covered the granite with a gray sheet and had sprinkled rose petals all over the top. Red, yellow, and white petals made a carpet of silky fragrance. The lit candles on the stove flickered and illuminated one side of Jordan's face, while the other remained in shadow.

He handed me a wine glass filled with water. A little fancy for water, but it suited the setting. The water soothed my parched throat. Imagine screaming at a football team for a few hours. That's what a few minutes with Jordan did to me.

I picked up a petal and sniffed the subtle aroma. Even though this was a kitchen, Jordan had created a completely new romantic nook.

Once I finished the water, I handed him the glass. Behind my back I heard the clink of the glass being set in the stainless steel sink.

Upon returning, he carried another glass and a bottle of Syrah. I love Syrah. I love red wine. To be honest, loved all wine and the more the better, so I was pretty darn happy when I saw the bottle. "We get to drink wine?"

"No."

My heart sank. "Then why tease me with my favorite?"

He poured a glass and smiled. "Not for you to question. Now lie back."

I did. It wasn't like we hadn't fucked on the counter before, but somehow I had a feeling this would be different.

The sheet protected me from the cold granite, but the flowers were a bed of cool silk to my back. The essence of rose surrounded me, and I inhaled a deep cleansing breath that filled my head with their delicate fragrance.

Jordan circled the counter with the glass of wine in his hand. He never took a drink, and our eyes locked on each other. "You like wine, don'tcha?"

"You know I do."

"You'd probably take a bath in it wouldn't you?"

"If I'd have thought of it, yep."

He tipped the glass and several drops splashed on my belly. Even though the wine wasn't cold, the contact with my aroused body spread icy chills. He poured even more drops on my pebbled nipple. The drops pelted my sensitive nub and had a similar sensation to wax. I cringed from the cool liquid but felt elated almost immediately.

He poured a line down the center of my body. The wine puddled then trickled over my sides making me want to brush away the tickling juice. He refilled the glass and continued to drizzle a fifty-dollar bottle of California central coast wine all over me.

I adjusted to the cascading grape train until he aimed the stream to run into the *spot*.

Shit. That felt crazy weird and glorious.

Jordan set the glass on the edge of the island and grabbed the bottle. Dumping the remaining wine from my pussy to my face, he made sure every drop landed somewhere on my body. Soon the sweet smooth wine would turn sticky, and I had a hard time getting out of my head there went fifty dollars' worth of wine.

I heard the buzzing of a lowering zipper, and my

heart raced. I sighed with relief. This little encounter had expanded to include him. Jordan climbed onto the island looking like a stalking tiger. He moved until his hungry gaze penetrated my eyes. His expression held no humor now—only lust and my breath caught in my throat. The tightly wound coil in my core edged up another notch.

He smiled and then moved lower.

Oh my God. Now I understood the wine. He began to lick every spot of wine left on my body. Short dab licks, long, slow laps that lasted too long and ended too soon. My body crackled with the electricity generated by each erotic swipe. When he'd absorbed every drop, he again unnerved me with his burning stare.

"I'm not a big wine drinker, you know, but I think I've found a way to enjoy it now." His low and edgy voice made me shiver with need.

He came down to my lips, urging them apart with his own. I tasted the sweetness of the wine and the essence of the man. Together they created the most delicious dessert ever. He devoured my mouth, swirling and dancing with my tongue, exuding his dominance. And I submitted because I fucking loved every single moment.

He pressed his body against mine burning me with his own heat. Then I welcomed the stretch as he filled me. I wrapped my legs around his waist and arms around his neck and hung on with each frenzied thrust. He'd waited until I had everything I needed before seeking his own satisfaction.

"Come on. Talk to me, Angel. Talk to me." He moaned and grunted every word.

"Push me. Push me. I can take it." I could. "I can

always take it." I gasped from his pressure on my chest and from my brain forgetting to tell my lungs to inhale. With each thrust, I lost more and more of the reality except for the perfume of rose and sex clouding over us. He stroked and filled me with his drug, and I took flight, floating on air, flying…

Ooommph!

Chapter Ten
Jordan

I struggled to breathe.

The cold floor tile pressed into my back. What in the hell had happened? I was about to nut—a wicked carnal nut and then we're flying through the air. Somehow, I managed to flip so Angel would be on top.

The force of us hitting the ground made me wonder if I'd broken my back. "Get off. Get off. Get off!" I didn't mean to sound so frantic, but holy fuck my back hurt. Angel scrambled off and kneeled beside me.

"Are you okay?" Even in the dim light, her eyes were moist with fear.

I wiggled my toes. Okay, I wasn't paralyzed. I moved my arms. That was good. "By okay. Yes, I don't think anything is broken, but as bad as this hurts now, I'm not sure I'll be able to get out of bed tomorrow." I swallowed hard and took a painful deep breath. "Get me a blanket, and I'll sleep here."

"For a brief moment, you were so good, I was hallucinating we were flying." She joked, but I still saw concern in her eyes.

I slipped my hand into hers and squeezed. "I'll be fine, and I am that good."

Her warm hand stroked my forehead. I hadn't hit my head on the floor, but her hand still felt good. I'd planned everything and all was fuckin' amazing until I don't what the hell happened.

"You know, I wonder how you managed to flip over so you wouldn't land on me." Without the heat from our sex, goosebumps popped all over her, and her nipples popped their sockets. If I hadn't hurt so much, I would've attached my lips instantly to one.

"Good thing I did or we'd be on our way to the hospital and trying to figure out a way to explain what happened."

Seriously? I was getting another woody?

"Angel, you might go put some clothes on. Lying here staring at your body is playing hell with my dick, and I have my doubts that trying anything again would be a wise choice."

Her slow cocky smile did little to help my condition. She possessed the golden goose and flaunted her trophy without mercy and with complete purpose. I was so deep into her it scared me. The thought of being without Angel terrified the hell out of me.

She leaned over me—her lips hovering millimeters above mine. "Whatever you say, Sir."

Fuck me. I closed my eyes. Her whispered breaths teased my lips. She never kissed me, but she sure as hell caused a huge knot in my groin.

She left and I painfully maneuvered my body to a sitting position. "Down, will ya?" My dick stared hard at me. "Not happenin'. Come on, help me out here. I'm in enough pain."

I managed to walk to the sofa, but not without a litany of old man sounds. I sat with my bare ass on the cushion until Angel returned in her pajamas. She carried with her a pair of gym shorts and one of my scores of university T-shirts.

"Are you sure you're okay? I mean you don't look good at all." She tossed the clothes in my lap. "You want me to help you?"

She didn't say it to mock me. Her concern was genuine. She had a smart mouth and weird sense of humor, but Angel's empathetic nature always overrode any joking.

"I got it, I think." Once I had the shorts to my knees, I had to decide whether to stand and pull them up or try to shimmy them on without raising my ass too far from the sofa. Opting for the shimmy, I had to grit my teeth and hiss a lot of *fucks* before the shorts were in the right place.

I laid my head back against the sofa and covered my face with the shirt. The cushion sagged beside me. I caught a hint of rose and wine before feathery soft fingers began circling the top of my thigh. Lifting the shirt, I peeped from underneath and smiled at my girl.

Tossing the shirt on the floor, I slapped my legs motioning for her to sit in my lap. She narrowed her eyes at me. "I don't know if that's such a good idea."

"I've changed my mind. Trust me, it's exactly what I need right now."

She eased slowly and carefully in my lap. Internally, I cringed, clenched, and coaxed myself into not crying, but I needed her close. Feather soft cotton of her pajamas brushed my nipple when she snuggled and lit me on fire. This was a bad idea.

I rested my chin on top of her head while her racing heartbeat absorbed into my own pulse. Two frenetic souls wondering what the hell happened.

"I think the sheet made the counter slippery," she said. "I mean before when we've done it on there, we flopped around on the counter. I think it was the sheet." She let out a sigh. "But the rose petals and all…that was a nice touch. I was pretty much loving it until what I thought was a fuck hallucination of flying went south."

She broke contact with my chest and stared at me. Her eyes shined with mist. "Are you sure you're okay?"

"Three or four Ibuprofen and I'll be good to go."

"Jordan. I don't mean your back. You've been different…like preoccupied with something."

I hope she didn't feel the tightening of every muscle in my body. "It's nothing really. I've some big projects going on at work." *It might turn into one big fucked up mess.*

I tipped her chin to me. "I'm preoccupied with making you happy."

"Well, that's a given." Angel had the most genuine smile of anyone I'd ever known. Unfortunate for me, she was also very intuitive, and I didn't know how long before this whole thing would blow up. I know I should have told her, but doing so would have me face the reality of what loomed on our horizon.

Chapter Eleven
Angel

I had a lot of empathy for Jordan when he old-man walked out of the condo. Whatever he had going on at work wasn't going to get any easier being in pain. I had work to finish as well, and should have showered off the dried sticky wine from my skin, but the warm cozies of remaining in pajamas overpowered my sense of cleanliness.

Freelance working didn't pay me near the money I'd made before, but the working at home had its perks...like staying in pajamas all day. However, for someone with focus issues, being at home was also a minefield of distractions.

My knees and ankles bore the red marks of my straining the shit out of the ropes last night. I didn't care. It was nothing long pants wouldn't hide, and I'd do last night every single night if we could...except for the falling part.

The weird thing is for a moment, I believed we were flying or at least suspended in air. I still possessed the remnants from the holy shit orgasm I'd had ten minutes before, so it didn't take much for me to have an outer body experience. With his furnace of a body amplifying his scent, I'd lost all sense of reality until we went crashing down...literally.

My phone buzzed with an incoming message. Bri.

—Lunch?—

—Only if I get off my ass and finish this manuscript by noon.—

—Then get off your damn ass and finish. I've got things to talk about.—

—Yes, Ma'am—

I had to admit Sabrina had become very un-Sabrina like in the last few weeks—since she'd met Cameron. She'd thrown piety overboard without a life raft and put the wanton boat into top gear. Can't say I was upset about the whole metamorphosis, more like startled to the point of pissing myself. I suppose I was to blame for their whole union, and my husband was none too happy about possibly having a lifelong connection to the person he despised. The one saving grace for him was that Bri and Cameron were moving to Chicago.

That fact made me nauseous. How could she leave me when we'd gotten back together? Which brought a smile to my face. I wished I could have been there when Bri told her parents she was moving to Chicago to live with a man she'd known but a few weeks. She loaded up her sin wagon to the point where I could picture her mother lighting candles every night and asking God whatever did she do to make her child go so wrong.

Of course, I knew the answer, and I would take it to my grave. However, the asshole smug part of me would love to see her mom's face if she found out her daughter's deepest secret. She never liked me anyway.

Me. Her mother always blamed any indiscretion Bri even thought about committing on my slutty tendencies. Even at our wedding, the woman kept eyeing my stomach looking for a sign I'd gotten knocked up and that's why I was getting married.

The whole thing sucked. I was happy Bri found someone. I didn't expect Cameron to be the one, but despite my husband's opinion of him, he was a good man. My selfishness was the problem. Plain and simple I didn't want her to move away. A feeling kept nipping away at a spot in my head—a feeling so vague, I couldn't even determine the nature to be good or bad. I knew something waited, and I needed Bri with me.

The lure of income motivated me to finish my project three days earlier. So, at eleven fifteen, I peeled the jammies from my sticky skin, hopped in the shower, and managed to walk out of my door by ten minutes before noon but still with damp hair.

The restaurant sat a five-minute walk from the canal and featured my favorite guilty pleasures like grilled cheese, sweet tea, and giant chocolate chip cookies. I intended to indulge in all three to feed my ravenous appetite that day.

Of course Bri already sat waiting in a corner booth. I'd assumed she'd ordered so I placed mine and joined her. The overhead lighting reflected off her rich red hair, and she shined. I always thought her pretty, but now, Bri was damn beautiful. I slid into the booth and couldn't hold back the smile erupting all over my face.

She wrinkled her nose. "What's so funny?"

"Funny? Nothin's funny. Getting regularly and thoroughly fucked has done amazing things to your appearance."

Big eye roll. "You're so funny."

"No, I'm serious. You may not have realized this, but hair looks its best right after an orgasm, and by the looks of yours, Cameron has certainly found your sweet spot."

Fire-engine red splashed all over her face.

"Don't be embarrassed. I'm happy for you. It's about time you chose your life and not someone else's."

"It's still very weird to me. Of all of the things I imagined getting me...you know...excited, *that* never crossed my mind."

"That?"

I also laughed at the narrowed eyes and pursed lips. "Geez Bri. You have to be able to at least say the words to yourself. Come on, it's me. Look who you're talking to. The whole 'it' as you say was new, and strange, and a little, no, a lot scary at first. But, Jordan was so sweet and patient—well, you gotta be patient married to me I suppose—he made everything right for me realizing kinky shit excited the hell out of me."

A dreamy schoolgirl stare bubbled on her face. "You're right. And Cameron's the same way. I kinda melt when he touches me. I can't understand why Jordan hates him so much. You were pretty vague in what you said before about him not liking Cameron?"

Oh boy.

"Yeah. I meant to be vague."

She gave me the *look*. I had to tell her. "Here's the thing. Please don't take this wrong or think something different about Cameron because this is all in the past."

By her pained expression, she seemed ready for me to tell her that her boyfriend had secretly murdered someone. "It's nothing bad, really. See, he and Jordan's known each other awhile and frequented the same kink groups. Jordan has this real aversion to causing a lot of pain, in the form of whipping for spanking, hitting like that. More than a few times, the subs that Jordan was with wanted him to do those things…pretty hard. He didn't want to, and so they would leave him and go to someone else—that someone was Cameron."

Her mouth formed an "O," but no words managed to escape. Obviously, she knew Cameron wasn't opposed to giving them what they wanted because that's what he was doing when she walked in on him at the party.

Even though I'd known awhile, I still didn't quite grasp why Jordan still held onto that grudge. I'd always thought men got shitty at each other, then moved on. I especially didn't get holding on to that particular grudge because if they hadn't left him, we wouldn't have even met. I'm the one who should be shitty…and at my husband, not Cameron. Part of me believed this was still an issue because Jordan knew I thought Cameron was not only a nice enough guy, I thought him attractive. Damn. I was married, not dead.

After a few more fish-mouth gestures, Bri found her voice. "I did not think…I mean I know he's okay with…" Red hair and red face made for an interesting combo. "You like it, don't you? I'm just…I don't know. I'm not sure what to think about spankings. I think I should be ashamed, but…"

"But you're not." I knew how she felt. This was a big deal. I never thought I was a slut like Bri's mom thought I was, but I had way more of a sexual history than she did. And I know how weird kink seemed to me then. I could imagine how earth-shattering Bri found her thoughts realizing she got a lady woody from a red ass.

"Honestly, Bri. I'd be more concerned that you want to move in with him this soon than I would be that you think sex can be fun." I saw the server approaching with my lunch, and so I thought it best to stop the conversation for the briefest of moments.

"Okay, so has your mom and dad calmed down any?"

Her pained expression forced a lump to lodge in my own throat. We were both only children, so I understood disappointing parents or in my case, parent. Although, in my defense, I went the more traditional route and married Jordan before I actually moved in with him.

"I have to say that it is a refreshing change that you are now the bad girl in this relationship. In all seriousness, Bri, we're old enough to make decisions based on what we want and need and not on what our parents will think." I tore a piece of gooey grilled cheese from the sandwich and savored the heavenly velvet rolling around in my mouth.

"If you're happy, then the decision is right." I reached across the table, cheesy fingers and all to grasp her hand. "Are you happy with your decision?"

Like a curtain on opening night, a smile slowly spread across her face. "Crazy happy. Does it sound weird I feel very safe with him?"

"You should feel safe with anyone you have a relationship with."

She stared at the table, but I saw a slight smile. "He's taking me somewhere special Friday, but he won't tell me where."

"And you think he's got something special to ask?" My own stomach filled with butterflies, I could imagine how she felt.

She shrugged. "I'm not totally sure, but he's

already asked me to go to Chicago with him. What else could it be?"

I told the stomach butterflies to simmer down. I had to be the voice of calm and reason. *Oh please, you can't even say that with a straight face.* "Maybe he's found a really terrific place for dinner. Don't be too disappointed if…oh hell, I can't do it. I think you're getting engaged."

She beamed. "Do you think so? I mean, for sure think so?"

"Normally I'd say 'no,' because you've only had this ever so odd relationship a few weeks, buuutt, this whole thing has been weird enough that I think you're getting engaged."

Cameroon never seemed to me to be the kind of guy who was interested in being married, but my Bri had some sort of magic power to have changed his mind. I was certain he'd give her a ring or I wouldn't have encouraged her. "Sabrina, stop bouncing."

"I can't help it. But, why do you think he'd do it so soon?"

I popped the last bite of grilled cheese into my mouth. "Mmm. Well, moving up there with him's kinda a big thing for you. Maybe, he wants you to be confident he's serious about the two of you."

"It'd definitely make my parents happier."

I hadn't said a whole lot about their beliefs, but I didn't like the way they pounded purity into Bri's head. "I'm going to say this at the risk of pissing you off, but considering your dad fathered a child out of wedlock, I don't think they have very solid ground to stand on."

She chewed the inside of her lip, and I wasn't sure what her next words would be. "I know, but that happened when Dad was in the navy before he and mom met. He didn't even know about him until last year."

"Still, though. Have you met him?"

She sucked the last few ounces of her drink through the straw until the cup gurgled empty. "No, saw photos, though. He lives in California. Dad's met him. Mom's not real keen on having a stepson. He's kinda hot though." She blushed. "I know. That's creepy, but it's not like we really know each other.

"Well, I probably shouldn't be commenting on your hot man."

She laughed. "I'm telling Jordan."

"Current mood of his considered, I'm asking you not to."

I meant what I said as a joke, but Bri turned very serious and pale. "What's wrong?"

She swallowed a few times and began winding her hair around her fingers. "I probably shouldn't tell you this, but you're my friend and you should know, and I don't know what to do."

"What are you talking about?" A weird sense of dread settled in my stomach.

"When I said I saw Jessica Forner at Koffees. She wasn't alone. She was with Jordan."

Chapter Twelve
Angel

Two fifteen, three twenty-three. Four thirty. For me, fury slowed time.

I could have called Jordan at work, but I did have sense enough to know hashing this out over the phone was a bad idea. No, I wanted him home because over the phone I didn't have the ability to knock the living shit out of him…or at least try. Why in the fuck did he not tell me about him being with Jessica?

We hadn't had a big ugly fight in a long time, and this would be ugly.

I expected him around five thirty. So in the forty-five minutes between five thirty and the time he actually opened the door, my demeanor got a whole lot uglier.

As soon as we made eye contact, he knew I was very pissed about something.

"Angel. Hi. How was your day?"

I crossed my arms, and the kitchen island supported my shaking body. "Interesting."

He hesitated. "As in?"

As he bent to kiss my cheek, I moved away from his aim. "Something I never expected."

He shrugged out of his jacket and threw it across the counter. "Why don't you stop being so cryptic and tell me. I don't feel like playing games. Not a good day."

"I bet it wasn't. Going all day knowing you lied to me." Still he stood there like he didn't know, and his lack of acknowledgement crushed me.

"Angel, please. Stop dancing around and tell me." His eyes bored into me, daring me to call him out. He knew. He fucking knew, but waited for me to say it like he needed time to design a defense.

"I don't really feel much like your Angel right now, but the man I thought I knew would have told me he'd talked to Jessica Forner right before she was murdered. You know how sick that makes me feel?"

"How did you find out?"

The pounding in my head neared the point of explosion. "That's what you're concerned about!" Not *why did I act like her death was no big deal*? Or w*hy didn't I tell the person I'm supposed to be completely devoted to*? "Why, Jordan? I don't understand this at all. Why did you talk to her when we decided it wasn't a good idea?"

No longer did I see the man who could control every moment of my sexual desire. I saw a man with fear in his eyes. What I didn't know was it a fear of what he'd done or a fear of what could happen.

"I thought I could talk her out of publishing the story. I thought she might have one shred of decency, but she didn't. I was even going to offer her money. We didn't even talk that long. She got up to leave and I wanted more time to convince her." He scrubbed his head with his hands. "I reached to stop her, and she clawed my arm."

The scratch on his arm.

"Then she left, and I saw Sabrina, and realized she

witnessed the whole thing. I asked her not to say anything, but…"

"She's loyal to me, Jordan. She didn't tell me to get at you. She told me because she thought I needed to know. She's right. I need to know. What if the police come, and I didn't know anything about it?"

"That's what I wanted. I didn't want you involved."

"Involved. Jordan, this whole thing is my fault to begin with." The entire room turned hazy and red before my eyes. Nausea consumed me, and keeping the contents of my stomach intact consumed the few remaining ounces of energy I had remaining.

"You couldn't have known what she would do."

"And you did?" *Why would he not have stopped me?*

"I didn't actually think this would happen. I feared but still a little shocked." He shoved his hands in his pockets and rested against the counter. "I'm sorry. I'd do anything to protect you, and I've made it worse."

"What do you mean?" What could possibly be worse than he lying to me could?

"She scratched me deep enough to draw blood. That means my DNA is or was under her nails. I guess this all depends on whether she cleaned up before she died."

"That's why you didn't want to go to the police."

"That's why. I'm hoping the trail leads somewhere else other than us."

At six foot five, my husband now seemed very small and vulnerable. He'd made a choice for my benefit, and now, the wrong decision had bit him in the ass. I was still angry, but I couldn't build a wall between us. Neither of us could deal with this alone. I went to him and wrapped my arms around his waist. Resting my head against his chest, I smelled the stress of the last few days permeating his shirt.

"I'm still mad at you. I understand why you didn't tell me, and I love you for loving me that much, but we've got to be there for each other, Jordan."

He kissed the top of my head and whispered. "Yes, we do."

I squeezed harder willing his heat into my body. "No more secrets?"

"No more."

Chapter Thirteen
Jordan

Fucking hell.

How could I have lied again three seconds after closing out the first one?

Telling her where I really was all week, may have been too much. I hated every minute I spent there. I'd been doing this before we were even married. Keeping clients happy was part of my job. That's how I justified not telling her after we were married. I moved on—another deflection I suppose, but one we both needed.

"You want to go away this weekend?"

Her dark eyes were warm now and not the wicked fiery of a few minutes ago. "Away? Where?"

"Where, is my surprise, but I think you'll like the place."

"If you don't tell me, I won't know what to pack."

"You won't be choosing anything. I'll give you a list of whatever you need."

"Is this going to be a session?"

"Seventy two hours' worth. No decisions. No choices, and no reprieves. Interested?"

Her heartbeat pounded into my chest. We needed this weekend to repair the trust I'd violated. I prayed she didn't notice the cold rushing through my body.

"I might be a little bit interested…maybe more interested if I knew what hotel we were going to." Her fingers began unbuttoning my shirt. With each button, the crotch of my pants grew tighter. By the time she reached the bottom, I'd be in pain.

"We're not going to a hotel. We're going to a cabin." Mark gave me details about his property, and I couldn't wait to use them on Angel.

When Angel's hands invaded the cavity of my now open shirt, I flinched. I was ashamed to admit, I had little control when she touched me—one of the best reasons for binding her hands. That and keeping her arms behind her pushed her breasts into glorious display. Nipple clamps made her chest heave in such rhythm I had trouble focusing from its hypnotic effect. Her cries when I released them sounded more orgasmic than painful. "A cabin." Her hands continued to skim up and down my back. "Where? How much did it cost?"

Gripping her forearms to stop my torment, I said. "Free. Someone is letting us use it."

"Why the mystery? Who?"

I feared if I told her, she'd be on the phone tomorrow asking Laura the details of the place.

"Oh come on. Tell me."

I might have had kept her fingers at bay, but staring into her face with her curls creating a frame for those dark lashes and amazing eyes, melted my resolve. "Mark and Laura have a rather isolated cabin in Brown County. We get to spend the weekend there."

I released my grip from her arm to grasp her chin. "And you better not be calling Laura to ask about the cabin. Mark made it clear to Laura not to tell you anything." I squeezed a little tighter. "And unlike you, Laura actually does what Mark says."

I wiggled my jaw. "Apples and oranges. Besides, they're doing a twenty-four/seven thing for a couple months."

He scoffed, "Maybe we should try that."

"Maybe we should file Be like Mark and Laura in with the waxing the pubes section."

I kissed the top of her head. "Another time maybe."

I turned from her to walk to our bedroom, shedding the shirt Angel already opened. The very instant I kissed her head, the scent of her shampoo invaded my nose, and the very possibility I could lose that sensation rattled me.

"Jordan?" She called after me. "What's wrong? Are you okay?"

Shirt in hand, I turned to see her beautiful confused face. "I think I want to lie in bed for little while." I opened my palm in invitation. "Come with me?

"Always."

Chapter Fourteen
Jordan

I couldn't remember the last time Angel and I spent time in bed not sleeping, making love, or fucking. Until now, I never realized how beautiful the feeling was holding on to someone you love. Granted, I still had a major hard on, but with Angel tucked in my arms, I knew, without a doubt this was all I truly needed in life.

The sight of her struggling in her bonds and responding to my every touch excited me beyond words, but take away the ropes, the straps, the "Sir," and even the collar and still I'd lay claim to being the luckiest man on the planet because I still had my Angel.

That's what scared me. I could lose those moments. I could lose the freedom to ask for her submission. I could lose everything important in my life. Whether or not I confused my wife with my lack of sexual activity, I didn't notice her to be frustrated. Her body melded into mine—her back relaxed against my chest and her breathing became even with my own.

She had no way of knowing how scared I was. I couldn't tell her where I was or what I was really doing that night. Everything depended upon my silence, and my silence may very well destroy us.

"Jordan?" She shifted in my arms but snuggled again.

"What is it?"

"Are you scared the police will come talk to us?"

I closed my eyes and ruffled my lips through her hair. "I'm certain they will."

"You think so? I mean even if they do recover DNA, how would they know to check you? I didn't get the impression anyone else knew what she was doing."

"Her boyfriend knew. Remember? He came to the hotel with her and waited in the lobby."

"Damn. I'd forgotten about that."

She broke from my embrace and turned to face me. A flicker of an idea flashed in her eyes. "Maybe her boyfriend killed her. You know they say most murders are committed by the spouses or significant others. What do we know about him? He could be a real ass or maybe she was an ass to him."

"That's a lot of speculation, Angel." I caressed her cheek with my back of my hand. "But maybe you're right."

She grasped my hand with hers and separated my fingers as she began to suck on my index finger. The mere act of her touching me with her tongue reignited the erection that had begun to wane. She stopped sucking but the saliva from her mouth dribbled down her chin.

"Besides, Jordan. We shouldn't worry too much. You have an alibi. All you have to do is give the police the names of the men you were with. That would end the whole thing."

If only I could.

"So we shouldn't get too worried about it." She wiped away the moisture from her chin and propped her head on one elbow. "So, are you going to tell me anything about our upcoming weekend?

Chapter Fifteen
Angel

Since Jordan's packing list for me for the weekend amounted to my black lace corset, the black silk nightgown and matching robe, lacey underwear, and my hooker boots, I deduced we wouldn't be doing any hiking in the woods while at the cabin.

Also, he made it clear I was to give him my cell phone once we got on the road. Which meant, I had to notify anyone who might text me, that I'd be unavailable during the weekend. I had a feeling this locked weekend session would test my limits.

I got wet considering the possibilities.

When I'd found out Mark and Laura were doing a twenty-four/seven thing, I couldn't believe they would try something so strict. I mean being subjected to your Dominant's every whim at all times seemed not only exhausting, but annoying. However, Laura was a much better submissive than I was. She seemed to have no problem following Mark's instructions.

I considered myself lucky Jordan was so easy going. I mean, we had a much more rigid routine now than when we first got married, but still, these locked weekend sessions proved difficult for me despite the crazy overwhelming fucking reward. I still had trouble keeping my mouth shut, or not questioning Jordan's instructions. Hell, if he intended this weekend to be completely submissive on my part, he would have to keep me gagged the whole time.

Five minutes after I began packing, I had everything, including my toiletries packed into a backpack.

I didn't like the tiny little bag holding my entire weekend inside. The contents screamed we wouldn't be going to dinner, to a show, to anything with people in attendance. I wondered how far away from civilization was this cabin? For some reason, I kept running the storyline of Beauty and the Beast through my brain. Isolated with someone else making all the decisions and me along for the ride.

The fucking ride of my life, I envisioned.

When a loud knock burst my fantasy dream bubble, I needed a moment to slow my horny breathing before opening the door.

I wished I hadn't opened the door.

A man in dress pants and jacket stood on the other side of the door. He looked to be in his late forties from the sprinkling of gray in his close-cropped brown hair.

"Mrs. Caldera." He flashed a badge. "My name's Detective Rausch." He shifted his weight as if preparing to move toward me. "May I come in and speak to you a moment?"

Shit. Shit. Shit.

A shiver traveled up and down my spine activating beads of sweat under my hair. Another nightmare about to begin.

"I uh, I, yeah, I don't think so right now. I need to talk to my husband first." Pretty much sounded like a confession to me. "What I mean is, I don't know the legalities here, and I should find out first." Well that sounded even better.

"Mrs. Caldera, I've already spoken to your husband, and he said you would be fine talking to us," the detective said. "May I come in?"

I slipped from the doorway to the hall, closing the door behind me. "Regardless of what my husband said, I don't let strangers into my home. So what is it you want to talk about?"

Rausch's eyes bored into me. "Jessica Forner."

"What about her?"

"I'm sure you heard she was murdered. I want to know about your relationship to her," he said as he reached into his suit coat pocket and produced a small notepad with a pen slid through the spiral metal rings.

"I wouldn't say we had a relationship. We met one day to talk about something." My knees were losing their ability to support my weight. I leaned against the door as casually as I could.

"What did you talk about?"

"A story she was thinking about writing."

"What kind of story, Mrs. Caldera?" Rausch held the pen to paper waiting for my response, but he didn't look me in the eye.

He already knew.

Then I realized if the detective had talked to Jordan, he would have called me as soon as the guy left. I called up every ounce of bravado I owned, straightened my knees, and no longer used the door as a crutch. "I'm going to stop this conversation, go back inside. I'm not comfortable talking when no one else is around."

With my hand behind me on the door, I twisted the knob to escape this interrogation.

"Mrs. Caldera," called Rausch. "It's very important you speak with me. Better here than somewhere else. Don't you think?"

"I don't have to talk to you because I think you lied about already talking to my husband. I don't like liars."

I rushed inside and slammed the door behind me, once again needing the support of the sturdy wood. A deluge of tears gushed over my cheeks and pelted my chest. This was all my fault—not Jessica dying, but the police would never have showed up if I hadn't given her an interview. We had the perfect motive, and Jordan trying to fix the problem may have made the whole thing worse.

My selfish attitude, which almost destroyed Jordan and I once before, may have struck again.

"Dammit." I banged my fists against the door. "It's always about you, isn't it?" I kept pounding until my hands were numb. "Jordan will do anything for you and now look at what's happened."

Screaming at myself did little to ease the turmoil swirling inside my body. I wiped my eyes with shaking hands to prepare myself to call my husband about the detective's visit. Since I was relatively sure Jordan hadn't talked to him, I was now sure Rausch was on his way to his office. I needed to warn him. Going to his office seemed like bullshit to me, but I wasn't a cop trying to solve a murder.

I retrieved my phone from the bedroom, and for the time being, ignored the text from Sabrina. Her big night with Cameron was approaching, and now wasn't a good time for me to be excited for her. I'm a shitty selfish friend too.

Punching redial on his recent calls, I held my

breath, waiting for Jordan to answer. As soon as his velvet voice came on the line, I lost control and blubbered into the phone. "Jordan, a detective was just here."

Chapter Sixteen
Jordan

With the crying, I couldn't understand anything she was saying. "Angel, calm down. I don't know what you're trying to tell me. Are you hurt?"

Even though I didn't know where she was, I had one foot out of the door of my office ready to go to her. After one huge sniff, silence replaced hysterics.

"Angel? Are you okay? You're scaring me."

Her voice returned to something I could understand. "A detective was here."

Shit.

Not that I was surprised, but I thought they'd come to me first. Even though my job wasn't listed under Fairland Entertainment. Fairland existed as a subsidiary of Vander Corporation and sorta flew under the radar most of the time. But I suppose cops had a means of finding anyone. "You didn't talk to him did you? Legally, you don't have to."

Silence.

Shit.

"I started answering his questions because he said he'd already talked to you and you said it was fine. Then, I started to feel really uneasy about it because I realized you would have called me. So, I dashed back into the apartment and slammed the door."

A nausea began building in my stomach as I

walked to the window of my office and stared at the cityscape. Guilt or innocence had nothing to do with anything right now. The mere fact that someone had seen Jessica's story created an anonymity problem. "You did the right thing. Don't answer the door if he comes back."

I wanted to go home to her, and as soon as my conference call meeting ended, I was out the door. I also needed to find a lawyer. I needed…

"Mr. Caldera?"

I jerked my head to the unfamiliar voice. A stranger lingered in my office doorway. This had to be the guy who invaded my world. "Yes. May I help you? I guess my admin isn't at her desk?" At least if Karla had been there, I'd had a few seconds to compose myself instead of him walking straight to me.

"No, no one was there. May I speak to you about something?"

"And who are you and what do you want?"

"I'm Detective Rausch from the Indianapolis police department. I'd like to ask you a few questions about a crime."

I don't know if I was pissed at him for being here, pissed at myself for the reason they were here, or pissed because I had no control over this situation.

"What crime? I don't know why you'd be here and especially don't know why you'd come to my place of employment. It's bad enough you go to my home and try to question my wife telling her I said it was fine."

"I thought you didn't know who I was or why I was here?" Rausch said.

"My wife called me very upset, and I don't appreciate that."

With an arrogant casualness, he strolled to my desk.

"Do you mind shutting the door?" I shoved my hands in my pants pockets

Rausch strolled back to close the door but returned all too soon, and a sick feeling compounded with every breath I inhaled.

"Mr. Caldera, I apologize for upsetting her. I had no idea a few questions would bother her so much."

I crossed my arms and rested on the window ledge of my view of state offices and downtown hotels. "I'm certain the police unexpectedly showing up at someone's home would be upsetting to anyone."

"Mr. Caldera, now you know I wouldn't show up unless I had a reason." Rausch crossed his own arms. His dark eyes connected with mine. He was a bulldog for sure, and even someone as tall as I was would not intimidate him.

He continued. "Jessica Forner was murdered a few nights ago, and while nothing directly points at you, a document open on her laptop had some interesting things to say about you and your wife, and your *interesting* lifestyle." A hint of a smile crossed his lips. "Were you aware of this document?"

I knew I had to end this conversation before I said something stupid. "I don't have anything to say to you unless I have a lawyer present."

"Mr. Caldera, I'm trying to gather information, cover all the bases. No one is, like I said before, pointing a finger at you. Why would you need an attorney?" Rausch slid his hands in his pants pockets and narrowed his gaze at me.

I pushed away from the ledge and planted my

hands on my desk. "As I said before, I don't have anything to say unless I have a lawyer present." I pointed to the door. "Now, if you'll excuse me, I have a meeting."

"Well, uh, thank you for your time," Rausch said.

As he turned to leave my office, Rausch glanced around and narrowed his eyes. "As the cliché says, 'Don't leave town,' Mr. Caldera. We may need to talk again."

I may have been speaking, but I know I held my breath the entire time he was there. As soon as he left, I collapsed in my chair. Tiny beads of sweat popped on my forehead, and I loosened my tie.

My whole body shook. Angel. How dare he go to her first and then lie to her. Good thing I extinguished my first instinct to pop my fist in his face. I needed to go home. I needed to find a lawyer.

"Jordan?"

I recognized the voice and not one I wanted to hear right now. I raked a nervous hand through my hair. "Yes, Mr. Levendar come on in."

In he walked. The only guy I had to answer to moseyed to my desk. He gripped a cup of coffee in his Big Kahuna mug and wore an uneasy smile.

"I saw a man I don't recall knowing leaving your office. Who was he?" He sipped the coffee—his eyes peering over the cup.

Could this day get any worse?

"Umm. A detective."

"Detective?" His voice projected confusion, but I knew the thinly veiled question meant 'What was a detective doing my building?'

The question became 'do I tell him the truth, be

extremely vague, or act clueless?' A fly caught in the spider's web pretty much described my terror. This man hired me when I was cashing unemployment checks. I owed him the truth.

I rested my elbows on my desk and tapped my clasped hands against my chin. "That woman, who was murdered…Jessica Forner. Well, Ang…Emma and I sort of know her, and he was asking about that."

"Sort of?" The deliberate slowing sipping of the coffee worked well as an intimidation tool.

"Sort of as in, she was writing a story about Emma and me which was supposed to remain citing anonymous sources, but that turned out not to be the case. She was going to expose our identities."

Bernhard Levendar knew about Cameron and me. He happened to be at a party one night both Cameron and I attended—a party where I lost another sub to that asshole. I don't think Levendar was there to participate. I think he was curious and knew the host. Cameron and I both thought he'd find a reason to fire us, but instead, we got extra duty. I'm still not sure if it's blackmail or we were best suited for the job.

He set the cup on my desk and moved the chair, making room for him to sit. "How do the police know about you and Emma?"

"From what I gathered, the story was on her laptop. I told him I wanted a lawyer present before I talked to him."

"Good idea."

"He talked to Emma first and told her I said it was okay she talk to them. I didn't. I didn't even know he was at my home. I'm absolutely furious."

"And you should be. Emma is a wonderful woman.

I'm sure this is quite difficult for her…for both of you." He braced his hands on the arms of the chair, pushing himself to stand. "I'll notify security that if he comes back to let me know first, and I'll decide whether to let him in. I can't guarantee I can keep him. If he has a warrant, there's nothing I can do."

He picked up his mug as if the thing were a cherished possession and fixed his stare directly into my eyes. "Jordan, you're my guy, but I don't want this interfering or causing any unnecessary publicity for this company."

I tried to swallow the huge lump in my throat. "Yes, sir. I understand."

I stood deciding at that very moment I needed help. "Mr. Levendar, I don't want to involve you in any of this, but I'm wondering if you could recommend someone who could find the right attorney for us?"

"I'll make some calls."

"Thank you." That may not have been the best decision, but going through the Yellow Pages seemed the equivalent of throwing a dart against the wall. Regardless of what the detective said and what I should have done, I refused to allow anything to interrupt the retreat I had planned for the weekend. We needed this. We needed the distraction.

I had so many ways to distract my Angel.

Chapter Seventeen
Angel

We talked little on our way to the cabin of the undisclosed location. Jordan came home from work two hours early, changed clothes, grabbed our bags—his much larger bag than mine—and we got the hell outta Dodge.

"Jordan, what did the lawyer say?" I can't stand silence.

"Angel, you know we've started…"

My hand went to the thin piece of leather around my neck. "It seems to be missing a vital piece."

"A mere technicality. I'm not putting a padlock on you when we're driving. You know, in case of an accident."

"For crying out loud, Jordan. This is important. What the fuck did the lawyer say?"

The knuckles of his hands gripping the steering wheel began to turn white.

"He said not to talk to the police unless he is present. Which means to call him if the police show up again or we have to go to the station."

"Oh."

Jordan turned his head to me. "That and his fee."

I hadn't thought of the cost. "And how much is his fee?"

I watched the swallow travel all the way down his

throat, and he let out a heavy sigh. "He was highly recommended. He's also highly expensive."

"I don't think bargain shopping an attorney is a good idea."

"You're right." He winked. I still melted like a schoolgirl, knowing the gesture was reserved for only me.

"We've other, more entertaining things to talk about later."

My heart leapt with joy. "I get to talk?"

"No."

"You're a real bastard. You know that?"

"As you've informed me several times."

****

By the time we wound through the twisting road with tree branches hovering over the lanes like a canopy, I began to wonder if we were still in the state.

"Jordan, he told you not to leave town, and we've been out of town for an hour."

He snatched my hand from my lap, his heat filling the chill that had crept into my body. "We're not that far, and I have my phone."

"He has your number?"

"No, but it's not that hard to prove our whereabouts. We got gas, and I have to stop by a caretaker's house to get the key." His focus never left the tiny road, but he squeezed my hand tighter. "It's fine, Angel. We need this time together. Even though we're not involved, things might get ugly for us."

The difference between being ashamed and being embarrassed had clear meaning lately. I shouldn't have had to justify my choices to anyone, but having the world connect our names to something so many found offensive or perverted…well, I would be embarrassed. I remember Sabrina's face when she found out. Her disappointment crushed me. Now, she understood, and wow, hopped into the life even faster than I did. I know though, she would be mortified if her family ever knew about her and Cameron's love life.

My husband was right. I'd better enjoy the weekend because inside I shook with the phrase "Who knows what tomorrow might bring," on repeat in my head.

I hadn't even noticed the car had stopped.

"I'm going to run in and get the key. Don't go anywhere."

I glanced around the area. The caretaker's house was a small single story home with a very country front porch. The house sat in the middle of a clearing surrounded by trees…lots of trees. *Where the hell could I go? I had no idea where we were.*

He returned with a shiny key and lecherous grin. I had to admit, I was a little wet. I might have been a little prejudiced, but my husband was ridiculously hot, and I couldn't wait to get to our destination…and the cabin, too.

Chapter Eighteen
Angel

When Jordan said an isolated cabin, I thought "Okay, off the road with lots of trees." No, he meant no one around, *no one*, except maybe the ghost of Daniel Boone.

"Is there electricity and a flush toilet? Because the last time I had to take a shit in a latrine, I swore never again."

Jordan rested his head against the headrest and closed his eyes. I swear he was counting. I had a perfectly legitimate question. I was a glamper, not a camper.

"Yes, Angel, there is electricity, running water, flush toilet, shower, and everything else you need."

"WiFi?"

One eye slightly opened and cut my way. "You won't have time for WiFi."

How could there not even be two minutes available for online? "You have to shower sometime."

I think he kept his eyes shut to concentrate on the tortures he had planned for me.

"I won't be showering alone," he said.

Unbuckling my seatbelt, I slid across the car console, squeezing myself between his chest and the steering wheel. Jordan opened his eyes, and perused my position.

"So you're serious about me not getting my phone?"

That damn eyebrow raise he'd perfected spoke volumes.

"This better be good is all I can say."

No sooner had the words left my mouth when this really large hand wrapped around my jawline and forced face-to-face, eye-to-eye contact.

"Better be good?" He growled.

We exited the car, and I carried my tiny bag of the weekend's attire up the stone steps to the rustic cabin awaiting our shenanigans. Two rockers graced the wooden front porch. Perfect for watching the sunset. However, I had my doubts I'd be admiring any glorious sunsets on the porch.

Once inside, my amenities fear faded. A soft glow of light from a modern kitchen only added to the quaintness of the cabin. On one end, the kitchen with stove, fridge, sink, microwave was picture perfect from a country life magazine, while the opposite end sported a stone fireplace, plush sofa and hell yes, a well-stocked wine cabinet. In between sat a table made of old wooden planks and chairs covered with red plaid cushions.

I guessed the two closed doors contained a bathroom and a bedroom.

"Mark and Laura have a nice place, don't they?" Jordan's smooth voice broke my assessment of our accommodations. His body loomed over mine while his fingers squeezed my shoulders and teeth nipped at the small leather cord around my neck.

"It's very nice. And extremely cool they're letting us use it."

"In exchange for us doing a demo at their next party."

Every muscle, nerve, and hair in my body tensed.

"Ouch." He clamped down on my ear lobe before he started to laugh.

"I'm kidding. No strings attached. However, if you are interested in doing…"

"I'm not."

Draping his arms around my shoulders, he hauled me against his chest, and my breath hitched from the strength of my gentle husband.

"Go get undressed."

"And put on what?"

Hot breath rushed into my ear. "There was only one part to that sentence."

I don't know why but a rush of nerves paralyzed me. The devil you know or the devil you don't know. I knew everything about my devil and the primal charge of fucktasy he delivered, but I didn't know the setting nor how my Prince of Darkness would enlighten me in the middle of nowhere.

With reluctance, I left the sanctuary of Jordan's arms and correctly chose door number two leading to the bedroom. The bucolic theme continued into the room with a king-sized log canopy bed displaying a blue and yellow patchwork quilt on the bed. Plenty of places to use restraints on that bed, I surmised.

One thing I noticed was the lack of air-conditioning in the cabin. I opened the two opposite facing windows allowing a cross breeze to flutter the sheer curtains. Sandal by sandal, slow zipping jeans, bra hook by bra hook, I disrobed, smiling to myself as I remembered the first time Jordan told me to undress.

My first experience with bondage started with my husband cutting my thigh with scissors because I failed to comprehend that "undressed" meant everything off including underwear.

When I completed my task, I stood before the full-length mirror hanging on the back of the door. My breasts didn't yet sag, but the day would come. I didn't have enough body confidence to parade around in a bikini. From the way Jordan, licked, sucked, and chewed on every available part, I was pretty damn sure his thoughts differed from mine. My hair. Short of shaving my head, the mass of dark ringlets would never be under any control. They made good handles for grabbing and yanking though. I closely trimmed my pubes. Jordan hadn't visited the waxing topic again, and I didn't doing mind the maintenance.

I turned my head slightly to see the long line of my neck—clear and smooth for now. By the time Jordan finished with me by the end of the weekend, the skin would resemble red latticework.

I drew a deep breath and turned the doorknob.

Let the games begin.

Chapter Nineteen
Jordan

When I heard the creaking of a metal door hinge, I held my breath. When she emerged from the bedroom, I couldn't breathe. Maybe she wasn't perfect. Maybe other people didn't see her as I did. No one would see her this way. Not my Angel. I constantly bombarded her with the request to indulge my inner exhibitionist only because I knew she was steadfast in refusal.

Over the years, I'd exhibited plenty with other subs, but Angel was different. I didn't care she preferred privacy for our intimacy. I loved her. I loved her so much the thought of being separated from her was too much to consider. Exhibitionism was her major button I loved to push. Her muscles tensed. Her spine went rigid every single time I spoke of her on display. She had to know by now I only said the words to watch her reaction.

There she stood with her hair—a flood of reckless curls with no destination, but on a journey full of aimless wander—tapping her nipples with every step.

Perfection.

Perfect for nestling my hands deep. Perfect for wrapping tightly around my fingers. Perfect for gripping and tugging her head back exposing the alluring column of her neck.

She started to walk toward me, and with every step,

my jeans became more and more painful. My dick desperately wanted out, but I had something to do first.

"C'mere, I have something for you."

Her smile radiated through me and she closed the gap until she stood but a few inches from my chest. I used both hands to dive into her hair, angling her head to face me before I bent to kiss her.

I started gentle and slow, but once I tasted her, I crushed her lips to mine and knocked her off balance enough she grabbed my hips. Her fingernails raked across my jeans while she pushed her tongue deep inside of my mouth.

"Oh, fuck, you taste good." I moaned. I attacked again, sucking her tongue, gnashing my teeth against hers. I rcleased her head and crushed her against my body to feel my cock straining against my jeans.

"See what you do to me?" The scent of orange blossoms tickled my nose. She always wore florals. Never overwhelming, Angel's subtle fragrance epitomized her whole essence—a tiny bud, but with the right amount of tender care, she bloomed into the most amazing flower. Strong and beautiful, but still sweet and soft. Knowing I was the one who brought her to this fueled my hunger for her deliciousness.

I stopped kissing her, and her body tensed for a brief moment. She knew what was coming. Her creamy bare shoulder waited for me. One gentle kiss before I bit down, marking her. She gasped and flinched, but buried her head into my chest. I kissed again and bit deeper, knowing these marks would be around longer than the weekend.

As I licked and sucked on her shoulder, my hands undid her tiny collar and stuffed it in my left rear pocket. The right had another occupant. Her slender, smooth, exposed column of her neck drove me wild. Too white, too smooth. I remedied the matter without hesitation, biting hard, two, three, four times and each time Angel's moans became louder, and she burrowed so deep in my chest, I swore her lips touched the inside of my heart.

"Aaahh." She moaned a mixture of her pain and pleasure only I understood.

She whimpered as she ran her fingers up my neck and buried them in my hair, and snorted her displeasure when I removed them.

"You'll never have any patience, Angel, will you?"

"Maybe when you're old and ugly." She cocked her head to the other side, exposing the unmarked satin of her skin.

"Enough," I said. "Like I said earlier, I have something for you."

I had to make space between us or I'd blow my wad through my jeans and never get to my back pocket. Angel possessed me. She claimed every ounce of my self-control, and the worst part of this spell was her knowledge of the power she wielded.

When I positioned her at my arm's length, I detected a shift from the heat of ardor in her eyes to the fire of her vexation at my interfering of her planned seduction. Still holding her at bay with one hand, I reached my free hand to my back pocket to retrieve her surprise.

"Hold out your hand." I let go of her shoulder as she extended her right palm.

Chapter Twenty
Angel

I heard the jingle before I saw what he placed in my hand. When I saw my gift, I had to tell myself to breathe.

A new collar.

Equal in width to the very first one I ever wore in my fledgling days of kink, but completely different.

Beautiful, if you classified items like this as such, and I did. A black and red tapestry design covered the outside, while supple leather lined the inside of the collar. A black burnished circular ring adorned the front, and the buckle and other hardware in the back sported the same black metal.

Jordan's low but commanding voice startled me from my enamored gaze.

"Turn around and hold up your hair."

Jordan plucked the new collar from my hand and waited for me to comply. As soon as I piled my hair high enough, I watched in blurred slow motion as he brought the collar to my neck. With each millimeter closer, my nipples tightened and popped erect. I gulped my last unencumbered swallow for what I assumed a long time. As he wrapped and secured my new gift, he whispered unintelligible words in my ear.

The building ache between my legs bordered on painful, which became excruciating when I heard the *click* of the tiny padlock. I don't know why the incendiary source my carnal thirst now came from was the very object I panicked over when Jordan first told me of his need. Maybe the bond we created from a piece of leather is the reason. All I knew for sure was my pussy was screaming for help, and I kept shifting my weight to ease the pain.

"Stop squirming," he said.

Easy for you to say.

His hand came around and he slipped his middle finger through the metal ring. He tugged as he caressed my jawlines with his thumb and forefinger. "Do you like your present?"

"Yes." I promised myself I would make every attempt this weekend to follow the protocol we created. "Yes, Sir, I do. I…"

Don't talk too much. Follow the rules.

"Tell me," he ordered with hot breath assaulting my ear.

"I love it. I'd wear it every day if I could." I smiled remembering how terrified I was before of going in public. Now, it was second nature—as much a part of me as my wedding ring.

"Then I'd never leave the house, and we'd end up being homeless."

The metal clicked against the anchor as he removed his middle finger and inserted his forefinger. The sound, amplified by its proximity to my ears, enveloped my body. Jordan made two light tugs, and my knees turned to jelly.

"Turn around, Angel. Let me see you."

As soon as I faced him, I'd won that round. The sheer joy I received from witnessing his lustful expression made me do the invisible fist pump. No one else in the world did that to him. That was the definition of pure power.

"Holy fuck, you're beautiful."

Every woman had those days when she thought she owned the mirror and days when the mirror broke, but me, I owned every fucking day because this man told me so, and he helped me believe I did possess a unique exquisiteness. My hair always in a constant battlefield of chaos made perfect ropes for grabbing and anchoring. I was tall enough that when I dropped to my knees, my mouth perfectly aligned with his dick. Nope, I wasn't symmetrically beautiful, but I learned to love and use what I had.

Jordan bent down to open his "tool" bag sitting behind the sofa. With the dim lighting, I couldn't quite see what he was choosing, but I did hear the odd sound of a chain. We'd never used any type of chain before, and like every time something new arrived, my horniness experienced a brief wave of anxiety. I had to bite my tongue to keep from opening my mouth and asking, "What the hell is that?" I was having a butt plug flashback.

He dropped the chain to the floor and came to me with the wrist cuffs. I couldn't hide my smile. The more I struggled against the restraints, the wetter I got. I had the feeling multiple orgasms were headed my way. I didn't wait for Jordan to tell me. I immediately offered him my wrists.

"A little anxious, are we?" He adjusted the cuffs tight enough I couldn't slip my hand out, but loose enough to be comfortable for extended wear.

I gave him a slight shrug, but inside I was

screaming, *I will absolutely die if I don't get some relief.*

I caught my breath when I heard rattling again. Oh, there was a chain—black like the ring on the collar. One end held a clasp. My gaze trailed to the other end in Jordan's hand. A red and black loop matching the collar completed the other end.

A leash.

I wasn't sure how I felt about being leashed. I'd submitted to Jordan on most things, well except for fucking in possible view of others. I licked my lips with uncertainty of what was about to happen. I could safeword, and we'd stop, but I'd let this play out for a bit.

"I can see in your eyes, you're apprehensive." His icy blues eyes burned with desire...and assurance. "What about me do you know without question?"

I swallowed, feeling the knot travel down my throat and rub against the new leather. "I can trust you and all your decisions."

The chain clinked when he brushed my cheek with the back of his hand. "And do you trust me now?"

"Yes, Sir."

He opened the clasp and attached the chain to the ring. He then released the chain. I jumped. When the metal links slapped my body, I wasn't expecting the glacial feel. The tip of the dropping leather loop tickled my bush and came to rest gently swaying between my thighs.

His finger hooked the chain, drawing the cold metal across my nipple. I squeaked. After the initial chill, my tit tingled from the sensation of the metal raking across my nip.

He repeated the action across my other nipple.

I swallowed hard and closed my eyes in an attempt to quell the storm gathering down below.

"Angel."

I know. The closing of the eyes is a no-no when face-to-face. So, I opened them to see Jordan with a smug "I told you so," grin. Nope, this wasn't humiliating. Agonizing, tormenting, intense…fucking awesome, but not in the least humiliating.

Two more times, he teased my breasts before moving on to torture me with the strap. With every circular swipe across my snatch, the chain rattled and the clasp twitched against the metal ring. In my current state of inflammation, the cacophony surrounded my head in an amplified storm of discord. Every instinct I possessed urged me to grab the chain from my husband's hand to stop the torture.

But, I didn't.

I fisted my hands at my side because my reward would overshadow my discomfort.

"Oh, my Angel is strong tonight." He brought the tapestried loop to my face, brushing the silky material across my cheek. I saw challenge in his eyes.

Hell, yes, I was strong, but the threads of my self-control rope had started to snap one by one until only a few strands remained. My jaw hurt from clenching so tight. I refused to talk. I refused to fail. At least one time, I would succeed and follow the rules.

"Undress me."

Which said to me, "free candy, dinner's ready, green flag." As much as I wanted to rip the shirt down the middle and claw my way up his chest, I didn't dare damage number twenty-seven in his cherished college

T-shirt collection. So instead, I placed two fingers from each hand under his shirt and I slid the material up his body. I worked my fingers on his abs and chest. I *happened* to brush his nipples with the tips of my fingernails. As his nips snapped to high alert, he let out an orgasmic groan resonating from deep in his throat, while I whipped the shirt over his head and onto the floor.

That's power.

My passion drove my eagerness to submit my body to my husband, but his response to my gifts boosted my ego over the moon.

Once the shirt disappeared, I waggled my tongue around his breasts before I trailed my licks between them and continued the descent until I dropped to my knees. A jangling from the chain clamored in my ears as it hit the floor. The ringing and weight of my newest attachment enhanced the painful ache between my legs.

Each inch I traveled, Jordan's muscles tensed and twitched.

I feared his stone cock would slap me in the face once I unbuttoned the jeans. I knew beneath the heavy denim he was commando. The whole time I maneuvered the button through the hole, we regarded each other—not with a languorous need, but rather an irrepressible desperate and exquisite obsession with the other.

I wondered if we'd still have the same reaction twenty years from now. For now, I lived in the moment, and one thing mattered now. One zip opened the floodgate of cock popping me on the nose before directly pointing to my eyes, daring me, taunting me, challenging me.

Not to brag, well, actually, yes, to brag, I give awesome head, so I had no reservations when I guided my mouth around his steel shaft. Confident and eager, I managed one lick and one suck before a tug broke my concentration. With my mouth still wrapped around his cock, I noticed Jordan's hand on the chain. I turned my confused face to catch his expression.

"Not yet."

Trying to swallow my disbelief, I almost deep-throated him. With disappointment, I released his dick and sat back on my heels wondering *what the fuck?* I had skills to use.

"Stand up," he said drawing on the chain, but his voiced quavered with rough need. "We'll get to me later."

As much as I liked the idea of his statement, I hated leaving work unfinished.

I followed him to the bedroom—chain clanging and loop bouncing between my thighs. I should have noticed but didn't, the leather straps wrapped around the cross pole of the canopy. Jordan unwound the straps two rounds, which meant the length would hold my wrists above my head, but not fully extended. Without a word, I stepped between the straps. I ceased to breathe and a brief moment of panic clawed at my insides. He attached each cuff to the clasp at the end of each strap. I don't know why, but the click sound which signaled my restraint, terrified me for the most fleeting of seconds.

"Panic attack over?" Jordan cupped my cheek with his palm. His hands so strong, yet gentle, reassuring, and adept. I leaned my face into his warmth.

"Yes, Sir."

He kissed my forehead. "I have something else for

you." He left the room, and when he returned, he kept the surprise behind his back. *Dear God, please not designer nipple clamps.*

Gauzy curtains fluttered and danced in the wind blowing through the window, but the humid breeze made my skin sticky and trickles of sweat began to slide down my neck. I hadn't noticed the humidity earlier, but earlier I wasn't being shocked from the electrical current also known as my husband.

With his hands still behind his back, Jordan came to me…one stalking step at a time until his prey swallowed hard at the menacing expression on his face. I knew something different was about to happen. The problem was, I had no clue to my impending sweet torture, and my left knee began to rock back and forth with nervous anticipation.

He glanced at my bobbling knee and smiled. "Some things never change, do they?"

Was this a trick question to get me to talk without permission? I called up every ounce of my mouth self-control to use for the weekend. I wouldn't fall for his wily trap this early in the experience.

My clenched teeth pained my jaw closed while my knee shifted into overdrive.

"Tell me."

My signal to speak. "No, they don't. You still scare the hell out of me at times."

"Why now?"

I licked my lips. "Because you're looking at me with an oddly wicked confidence." I swallowed again feeling the pressure of the collar against my throat. "And I thought I knew you well enough to comprehend all of your intentions. I've thought wrong.

He gave me a slight nod. "I see." Moving one step closer, he waited inches from my quivering body. "I'm going to give you a choice. Door number one for the unknown or door number two for the familiar."

I drew breaths deeper and faster, while Jordan's finely carved chest inflated like a butterfly breaking free of a cocoon. What did I want? I always loved anything he did to me. Familiar would have worked, but even the familiar had been unknown at one time. He never disappointed me, never harmed me in any way.

"Angel, if you don't choose, I wi…"

"One. One. I want one."

"Good choice, because I've been practicing."

Practicing? When, where, and with who?

My mind reader husband broke out in a broad grin and shifted his weight side to side. "I haven't been working late every night. I've been to visit Mark a few times."

When he revealed my choice, I had a light bulb moment. A long, black riding crop with a black triangular tip of leather rested across his palm. I'd begun to suspect Mark was the one who'd been administering the floggings. For one, because he appeared to be a master of all things kink, and two, he was one of the few men in the group Jordan trusted in everything where kink was concerned.

A naked man with a stiff cock, holding a crop. It didn't get any better than that. His compass pointed north mapping the most direct route to the aching between my legs. The steamy air accelerated my body temp to boiling, and my sweat changed from a trickle to a stream. In previous scenes, the crop hurt, but seconds after each stroke, I barely retained any governing rights over my orgasms…with someone else administering the smacks.

Now, my dream was on the verge of coming to fruition. Jordan would wield the instrument. Holy fuck, I questioned if there was something seriously wrong with me if the sight of a stick instigated an orgasm. So many times he'd told me he wasn't comfortable using crops and floggers. What had changed?

I knew I had to risk breaking the rule. "Are you sure about this? I mean for you. I'm definitely on board."

His posture straightened. "Are you questioning me?"

I became fascinated with the knot in the wooden plank floor to hide my profound jocularity of our exchange. Jordan never did anything half-assed. Like a snake about to lunch on a mouse, a leather tip attached to the black rod slid into my downcast view before resting underneath my chin. A firm pressure forced my head upright, and I bit the inside of my cheek hard to keep from smiling.

"No, Sir."

Seeing as how I would be facing him, when he connected with my available targets was definitely going to have an immediate ouch factor.

"You know why I asked Mark to teach me?" He traced my jawline with the tip sending a rush of euphoria through every vein in my lower body—so much so, I slammed my legs together and squirmed to get relief.

"Because he's the best?" I managed to utter with no air in my lungs.

"There's that, but…" Jordan wrapped his free hand

around the chain making it taut and mere inches from the collar. Like lighting the fuse for dynamite, every move of the crop from my jaw to my throat, to the space between my breasts, ignited a herculean arousal. If the crop ever struck my flesh...*shit*.

"I suppose you've figured out Mark was the one administering the strikes. I trusted both that he would do it properly and not harm you, but also there would be no confusion as to making it a threesome. I wouldn't share you with anyone."

Intense.

The icy blue in his eyes could cut diamonds.

A clanging of metal filled the room as he continued to bind his hand around the chain until he arrived at the ring. Even Jordan showed evidence of the humidity attacking his body. A light sheen of sweat covered his chest and glistened in the low light of the room. Sweat mixed with his soap created an aphrodisiac I didn't even need to drink. I ingested every molecule with each ragged breath.

He unsnapped the chain, letting the leash crash to the floor in a heap and proceeded to circle my breasts with the crop. When the flap rested on my nipple, an involuntary gasp escaped my lips. Smooth, cool leather coaxed my nipple to an almost painful pebble. In an instant, his wrist snapped. I heard a whoosh, then a stinging pain radiated from the side of my boob, and instinctively I jerked hard on the restraints, but the pain morphed into a horny adrenaline needing more fuel to sustain itself.

"When I was holding you while Mark was doing this, you'd get the most astonished, immediately followed by a serene expression on your face. With every stroke you shifted from one to the other in an instant."

He slapped my other boob harder.

"Yes, that look."

He stepped close enough he rubbed the wet from his cock across my belly. Now, I was forced to raise my head to see his face feverish with lust.

Not love.

Never had I questioned Jordan's love for me, and this picture of pure primal greed made us not husband and wife, not lovers, but two people who were going to fuck so hard it hurt—so predatorily, our flesh would retain the marks of frenzy for days.

He stepped back, and tapped the inside of my thigh signaling to spread my legs. My heart raced, and I tensed bracing for his next move.

Fuck. That hurt, but don't stop.

"I was jealous. I wanted to be the only one to give you that look...ever."

Each time he smacked between my legs, the *whoosh* sounded like a missile right before impact. The leather tip had to be slick with my juices. After the third time, he dropped the crop to the floor.

I presumed I was the entrée for a man acting like he hadn't eaten in weeks. Well, good thing I was a gourmet cook. He kneeled before me, knocking me a little off balance when he grasped my ankle bringing the inner bone to his lips. With my body wound so tight from the crop, when his lips grazed my skin, I flinched so hard, I surprised myself I didn't kick him in the face. "Sorry," I said.

He rewarded me with a quick nip. With each alternating bite and kiss journeying up my leg, he alienated my conscious choices. My body reacted purely without thought, reason, nor rhyme with endorphins numbing any suffering from the bites he bestowed without tenderness or mercy. Red and imprinted now, I would sport the purple and blue tattoos of my submission.

When I believed I could take no more of the sweet treachery on my spongy thighs, Jordan cupped my ass with hands and entered me with his tongue. I watched flashes of red, white, and pink swirl in my blurred vision from the psychedelic drug he orally possessed. When I began to see stars, I knew I had a tenuous hold on my control.

"Jordan, please, I can't. I can't wait anymore."

He stopped only to say, "Two minutes."

Two minutes?

"I don't have a fucking stopwatch on my pussy, dammit."

And there it was. I'd lasted less than four hours before opening my mouth when I shouldn't have.

A stinging slap on my tit jolted me into practical lucidity. Somehow, he'd managed to keep sucking my clit and grab the crop to smack a corrective measure into my brain.

Success.

No longer about to explode, I managed to calm down…for about twenty seconds. Every swirl, poke, and suck brought me again to the edge of the volcano. I wanted my hands embedded deep in his hair, but restraints held fast. I screamed my frustration mixed with the rapture of an impending orgasm.

Then the bastard stopped.

You can't keep doing that to me.

Worse than a mind fuck, and I hated mind fucks. However, my pre-judgment proved completely wrong. Jordan released my wrists from the straps.

"Put your arms around my neck." His velvet tone tickled my ear, melting my resolve once again.

With pleasure, Sir.

Like a python, I wrapped my legs around his waist, locking my ankles behind him. With his forearms cradling my ass, he carried me across the room as if I weighed nothing. His frenzied momentum came crashing to a painful halt, when my back collided with the log wall. My *oof* of both losing my air and the likelihood of wood grain permanently etched into my skin, did nothing to slow his drive.

When Jordan shoved two fingers inside me, I sucked in all the oxygen he'd emptied from my lungs. Sweet holy hell, the man had fingers almost as talented as his dick.

"Damn, I know you love that."

"I can't hold it. I can't wait anymore," Is what I said, but it came out more like "I, I, I ca, can, can't. I can't wait anyanyanymore."

"Then don't. Let her fly, baby. Let her fly."

I bit hard into his shoulder as I released all the energy layered in a nuclear holding tank. I heard Jordan's own moan from the vise grip I exerted with my legs around his waist. My quivering body clung to Jordan absorbing all his heat into mine, rolling the sweat fest into one giant river of slick skin.

The hair that wasn't plastered to my face grew in height from the moisture invading every strand in the summer heat.

I had not had time to recover before Jordan thrust

hard and deep. Once again, my back raked hard across the wood. More punctures, more scratches tingled my flesh. His fullness inside of me completed my existence, sealed my fate, and lifted my heart to heaven and back.

When he released, the velocity was so violent, I believed the possibility of his firing his wad like a missile through my back very real.

I hoped when he was ninety, he had the strength to hold me because I'd never let go of this addiction.

Chapter Twenty-One
Jordan

Heavy, sticky, and static air plastered our bodies together while Angel slept—her quiet snores the only sound in the early morning. I may have I fallen asleep for a while, but most of the night I wrapped myself around her body holding her so close I couldn't even tell who was sweating more.

In the city, the dark is different. No matter where you were, even the tiniest bit of light could find you. But here, in the country bordering the woods, the blackness encompassed everything. The cloud cover hid the stars and draped the moon in an ebony shroud. I spent the night feeling and memorizing every contour of Angel's body and counting how much time between her breaths.

I never imagined I could love one person with the intensity of an out of control fire. I'd always had an affection for my submissives, but I never had the intention of wanting to share the rest of my life with any of them. It's like Angel had this superpower to crawl inside my body and take absolute control over all of my emotions, and she did her magic the first time we met and every day since.

As the darkness evolved to the silver and grays of dawn, I eased my arm from around her waist. As I admired my handiwork bite-marks on her shoulders, something else caught my attention. Across her shoulder blades and down her back, cuts, scratches, and bruises covered her back. Some had already scabbed over, but others, the deeper ones still wet in the cut flesh. I lightly brushed my hand across her blemished skin. None of those were intentional, and I regretted I failed to consider the consequences of what I was doing with her back jacked against the log wall.

I began to kiss each cut and bruise I forced on her. Most every touch caused her body to flinch. My barrage of touch caused her to stir but not face me. "I'm sorry." I planted another feather light kiss on her spine wishing my touch would make the marks disappear.

"For what?" Her sleepy voice cut through the morning quiet, awakening the birds for their morning chatter and as if waiting for her arrival, a cooling breeze drifted through the open window.

I kissed another cut along her shoulder blade. She flinched even more when I swiped my tongue along the edge of the abrasions. "For destroying your back. I had no idea I was pounding you so hard against the logs."

I couldn't understand the muffled words she said into the pillow. "What'd you say?"

"I said…I liked it."

"I'd hate to meet you on a battlefield."

"Why?"

"Because you are bad ass."

Her body shook with a giggle, and she reached behind her to place my arm across her waist as I rested my hand between her breasts.

We fell silent listening to the sounds of early morning in the country. My stomach grumbled, and I thought about getting up and cooking breakfast, but the unison rising and falling of our chests lulled me to the edge of slumber.

"I need to tell you something." From the sudden rigidity of her body, she was afraid to tell me.

"All right." I blinked several times warding off the exhaustion creeping into me.

"I didn't get my birth control shot this month." She stopped breathing.

I poked the back of her knee with my own. "I know. Now, breathe."

I'd known for a while she'd not been to get her shot. I wondered how long before she told me. Three weeks. She didn't forget. I wanted an explanation, but I wanted her to address it first.

"How did you know?" My hand between her breasts warmed with Angel's own hand covering and intertwining her fingers in mine. She had her own way of distraction, but I sensed this gesture had more to do with reassuring herself rather than changing the subject.

"Well, every appointment, reservation, special day, or whatever, you write on the calendar. And when that activity is completed, you put a little check mark beside it." Pushing up onto my elbow, I leaned close to her ear. "There was no check mark, and every other day with something written down, had its little checkmark."

Again, silence overwhelmed the room. She still wore the special collar, and I'm sure she was uncomfortable because of the humidity. I should've removed the heat generating leather piece before she fell asleep, but I didn't. I had every right to demand her explanation, but I'd waited this long, so allowing her to face her own consequences was the best choice.

She rolled onto her back to face me. "Are you

mad?"

"Yes. It's not so much you didn't go get it, but more you were afraid to say anything. I'm mad at myself because you don't feel comfortable enough to tell me."

Tears welled in her eyes, and a rock-hard lump caught in my throat. I hated seeing her upset. "I'm okay with you stopping. I'm happy about the thought of having a family." Pressing my forehead to hers, the sticky sweet smell of her perspiration, sex, and a faint hint of orange blossom invaded my nose and headed straight to awaken my dick. "But I should blister your ass for not telling me."

"Do you think the police will come back?"

A sharp stab of reality stole any chance of visualizing my beautiful Angel as a mom. "I don't know. Maybe. Obviously the document on her laptop was like a neon arrow pointing to us."

"Whether or not the story was complete, I'm sure her notes and everything were there." She snuggled her steamy body into mine…her hot breath burning a hole in my chest. "I mean she figured out the truth because of my tattoo. I bet the police figured it out a lot faster."

Normally I'd be in pain from the hard on because of her movement, but her words drained any chance and quickly deflated the morning wood. I'd hoped this weekend we could be free of what was happening. "She would have figured it out anyway. It didn't matter what names you changed or didn't change, at some point, the truth was going to come out. It's hard to hide anything these days."

Something…a tear dripped onto my fingers, and my heart broke because I knew why. "Hey, stop carrying around all of this guilt. It is what it is."

She sniffed. "But you didn't think I should do it. And as usual, I didn't want to listen to you. And now look."

"They're doing their job. I'm sure they've questioned lots of people." I didn't believe my own words. I couldn't imagine someone with her personality or lack of ethics had many friends. The circle of suspects was likely much smaller than what I was telling Angel. But in the last few months, I'd perfected my ability to lie, and I hated myself for going against everything I'd preached to her about honesty.

Pushing away from me, she once again lay on her back. Her dark lashes fluttered as she stared at the ceiling. "Are we going home today?"

No, we're never going home. I want stay here with you away from the phones, TV, and civilization.

"Is that what you want?"

Our conversation had ruined her mood. I wasn't finished with what I wanted to do to her—what I needed to do for me. I needed to bury my dick so deep in her I lost my sanity. I wanted her begging me for her release, and I wanted to hear her call me *Sir* again and again. And the thought of marking her ass red now excited me instead of scared me.

Her eyes closed as if the question was too difficult to answer. With her eyes still shut, she muttered, "Maybe."

Throwing my best ammunition in order to continue our weekend, I played unfair with her desires. "You know, Mark and Laura have a St. Andrew's cross in the back near the woods."

Her eyelids flew open. "No shit?"

Chapter Twenty-Two
Angel

Monday morning, I was never so grateful to arrive home from anywhere. The hour-long ride home on my smarting ass seemed like an eternity. Every time we drove around a curve, and I'm sure at least one thousand, the shifting of my weight rubbed the tender skin and reminded me my husband had gotten over his ambivalent feelings about whipping. I fell in love with the St. Andrew's cross as the moisture danced across my red ass. I loved every stinging stroke—the lingering effects, not so much.

Apparently, Jordan noticed my discomfort. "You want me to rub some stuff on your butt?"

"No, because it'll lead to something else, which'll make it worse."

He tossed our bags on the sofa, and with each step he walked toward me, the concern in his eyes grew deeper. "Is this still what you want?"

At first, the rain was a slight drizzle—a break from the humidity. I tested the bonds. Nope, couldn't move my wrists or my spread legs. Damn, we had to get one of these crosses.

Smack, the crop connected with the flesh of my butt cheeks. Ouch, but okay. The drizzle changed into a steady, cold shower with drops sharing pelting duty with the crop. Fucking ouch. I should stop this, but no.

Each time the leather hit its mark, after each flinch and swelling pain, the pressure of my arousal steamrolled until the agony of needing to come far outweighed the distress of the leather on my slippery, wet ass…

I wrapped my arms around his waist squeezing until his snug warmth surrounded me. Resting my chin on his chest, I focused my attention on his anxious stare. "In this case, the end justifies the means, totally."

I saw the relief flood through his body. He relaxed so much, I adjusted my hold to continue the hug. "I love every part of my kinky self with you."

"Me too."

He winked at me, and I went all gooey.

"I'm going into work for a few hours so I need to go change."

"You really like your job, don't you?"

"I do. Most of the time."

In less than fifteen minutes, he walked out of our bedroom looking all important and in charge. I watch people and make up stories based on their dress or actions. No story could I make up about Jordan better than the reality I knew.

"I'm not staying late, just finishing up some paperwork and answering e-mails. Shouldn't take too long, and then we can…"

A loud knock startled both of us.

Jordan opened the door.

Detective Rausch stood on the other side.

Chapter Twenty-Three
Angel

"Mr. Caldera, Mrs. Caldera, may I come in?" Detective Rausch made a move to enter our home, but Jordan stiffened. He understood the cue by his step back from the threshold.

"Not a good time. I was leaving to finish up some things at work."

Rausch glanced at his watch, not because he was checking the time, he had a point to make. "Running a little late aren't we?"

"Yes, I am. That's why I need to go. Now what can I do for you?"

His words oozed polite, but I knew in truth what he wanted to say was "What the fuck do you want?" Years of smoothing over difficult clients trained Jordan well.

"I'd like to ask you a few more questions about Jessica Forner," he said. "I think it'd be better if we do this inside."

Jordan kept a firm hand on our door. "I think it'd be better to have my lawyer present."

"What are you hiding that you need a lawyer?" Rausch asked.

"Look. I'm not stupid. I'm not playing into your little entrapment game. I know my rights, and if you have any more questions, we will do it with my lawyer present. Have a nice day." He slammed the door and slapped his body against the frame. "Fucker."

The soreness of my ass gave way to my trembling hands. This wasn't good. "Are you calling the lawyer?"

"Hell yes I am. I'd be stupid not to."

Chapter Twenty-Four
Jordan

Four hours

Four fuckin' hours that guy hammered me with questions, half of which my lawyer told me not to answer. Then I waited another hour for him to talk to Angel. Originally, they wanted to split up and question us both at the same time, but I wasn't going to let anyone talk to her without the lawyer which is exactly what the police wanted.

After numerous attempts to offer me water, I'd had enough of the false good host act and told him not to ask me again. Yeah, I wasn't offering up my DNA or fingerprints. They wouldn't let me talk to Angel before questioning her. It didn't matter if she accepted a drink or not. She only knew what I'd told her. It's what I didn't tell her which would be a problem.

Harry Luescher, our attorney, came with Mr. Levendar's highest recommendation. I wasn't sure why my boss had a criminal attorney on retainer, but I wasn't going to ask. Luescher's aura arrived before he did, and I wondered if I'd imagined the trumpet playing before his formidable image transformed from the blur of movement to the giant with black wavy hair slightly graying at his temples. Yes, I said giant. The guy was easy four to five inches taller than I was.

He reeked of success.

When I did a search for his dossier, his bio read like a How to Make Everyone Around You Feel Like They've Accomplished Nothing how-to book. Four years of University of Wisconsin basketball. Emperor of the Paint was his nickname. No surprise there. Graduated number two in his law class at Indiana University only because he missed six weeks of classes due to a rock-climbing accident. Passed the Bar the first time. Fucker probably aced it. My first impression of him and most every lawyer was he was an asshole. I didn't want a new friend. I wanted this to go away. He was my new favorite asshole.

He'd interrupted Rausch countless times with a refusal for his client to answer.

"Mr. Caldera is not on trial here." A red-faced Rausch gritted through his teeth. "We are only attempting to rule him out as a suspect."

"No shit?" Luescher produced the most grand and bogus smile I'd ever seen. "Sure seems like it…only we're missing a judge and jury, and you are making a very poor attempt at being the prosecutor."

Rausch's eyes bulged, and he went from red to a brilliant shade of scarlet. If my life weren't on the line, I'd found the whole scenario hilarious. But this show wasn't funny at all.

When he finally tired of Luescher's interference, Rausch told me I was free to go, but the hairs standing on my neck and the bones disintegrating in my spine suggested this was far from over.

As we waited for Angel to come from the restroom, we stood in uncomfortable silence, at least for me. Luescher examined the sleeve of his suit as if a piece of lint dared to fall onto the material. I didn't believe he was the kind of man who considered small talk part of the human existence.

"Do you think this is the end of it?"

He scanned the waiting area like he was preparing to talk to the United Nations. I stared at him with childlike wonder.

"No, Jordan. I do not." He paused. "They've zeroed in on you. It's a safe bet you're the only suspect on their radar."

A glacier of dread numbed my legs, and I snapped my attention to the floor to confirm I still stood on my own legs. "Umm. How, why do you think that?"

"Because water takes the path of least resistance, and from what you've told me, Jessica Forner sent you on a fast movin' river."

"Jordan?" Angel stepped into the bubble of our personal space. "Are you okay?"

I shoved my hands into my jeans pockets. "Yeah. I'm good. Let's go home." I offered my hand to Luescher. "Thank you for coming down here on such short notice."

"It's what I do. Don't hesitate to call again if you need me."

With a slight nod of acknowledgement, we parted ways. I snagged a secure hold on Angel's hand. I couldn't get out of there fast enough, and she stumbled several times trying to keep up with my accelerated steps.

I half expected a "Jordan, slow the fuck down," but I knew she realized I teetered on a dangerous cliff of sanity and stayed quiet.

Once in the car, I started the engine, cranked the AC, and sank in the soft leather of the seat. The noise blocked any sounds from the outside, and I took refuge in the cold blast attacking my sweaty skin.

"What did they ask you?" I hoped they didn't repeat the rapid-fire interrogation on her.

My icy fingers flinched when the warm touch of my wife's hand squeezed my own. "Uh, you know, um, where I was that night. Where you were. Why we were in contact with her in the first place."

"What'd you tell them? I mean about where I was."

Her thumb began circling and skimming the top of my hand in a hypnotic stroke. I closed my eyes and wished her touch had the power to make this nightmare go away.

"I told the truth. That you were out to dinner with a client. That's your alibi. That's easy to prove." The circling stopped. "That's where you were, right?"

I stopped breathing.

"Jordan? Right?"

Chapter Twenty-Five
Angel

"Jordan. Talk to me. What aren't you telling me?" A blazing white pain shot through my body, and I fought to draw a breath. A plastic bag of doubt threatened to suffocate me.

"Oh my God, did you? Are you the one who killed her?"

His eyes snapped open and he flicked away my hand. "How in the hell could you think that?"

"I don't. I know you wouldn't do that to anyone, but you weren't where you say you were. That I do know...now."

An instant shift into drive and the subsequent g-force of crazy acceleration bounced my head against the headrest. A twelve-block drive stretched for an eternity in the tense silence, and by the time we pulled into the garage, the pounding pain of his deceit threatened to explode in my head.

Why would he lie to me?

Once inside, Jordan collapsed on the sofa. I sat beside him, but he didn't or couldn't face me. He focused on the ceiling and rested his forearms on his head. "I didn't want to lie to you."

My heart dropped. The one thing I thought I'd never hear from my husband. "But you did."

"I did, and I regret it every single day."

"So this is a thing?" As if this situation couldn't get any worse. Yes, it's true. A person can see red. "So, if you're not taking these clients to dinner, then where are you going?"

I wasn't sure I wanted to know the answer.

"It's not every client, only certain ones…special, huge clients that bring in a lot of money, and we do go to dinner."

"But…" The throbbing in my head told me this would be a big 'but.'

"After dinner, I take them to the Heaven's Boat Yacht Club."

Hugging my knees to my chest did little to ease my anxiety, but at least I had something to touch that wasn't my husband. Resting my cheek on one knee, I asked the question I wasn't sure I wanted to know the answer to. "So, what's the Heaven's Boat Yacht Club?"

"It's an uh, it's an underground club, membership only."

"Is it a BDSM club?"

"Yes, but other things too. It's for people who want to have no strings attached sex in a controlled environment that's completely anonymous."

"People like…who are interested in cheating on their significant others?"

"Some, I suppose."

A metallic bitterness seeped onto my tongue and signaled I was biting my lip way too hard. "You suppose? So these clients you take there aren't married or involved. I find that hard to believe."

"Yes, Emma. Most of them of are married. Yes, they're cheating on their spouses. I don't like it. I don't condone it, but there's nothing I can do about it. Part of my job now is to babysit these assholes while they fuck without fear of discovery."

I tucked my hands under my ass for fear of acting on the violent urge boiling in my gut. "So, explain how this came to be. Was it in the fine print of your job description or did you ask for overtime?"

He stood and started pacing, raking his hands through his already disheveled hair all while failing to make eye contact. "One night, way before you, I was at a play party and Mr. Levendar came in. We were both a little shocked to see each other. The following Monday, we talked. It was no big deal. But then a few days later, he came to my office with a list of clients' names…some of our big bread and butter clients." Finally, he cast a glancing gaze my direction. "In addition to fancy dinners, they like *special* entertainment when they came to town."

He made two more trips along his pace line before chucking his back against the fireplace. "The HGYC is a very exclusive club. Levendar pays a chunk of money for the membership. He got tired of being den mother so now we get to do it."

"We?"

My jaw dropped, and Jordan's complexion drained from the red of embarrassment to the pallid hue of someone who let another cat out of the bag. The more I studied his face, the realization sank in. "Oh my fuckin' God. It's Cameron, isn't it?"

His hand shot up to stop the words he knew were coming. "Don't. Yes, Cameron was at the party, too and Levendar saw him. I seriously doubt he told Sabrina, especially since he's leaving. But that's for him to tell her…"

"Like you told me?" I couldn't believe what was happening. My husband, who expected me to tell him everything, hid this little gem of information from me. "I won't. And you know why, because my plate is already overflowing with shit I need to deal with. I'm not about to alienate my best friend again."

A part of me wanted to leave the safety of the sofa and wrap my arms around his waist and forget this nightmare, but a bigger part wanted to go to him and take a bat to his head. "So, in your life as a high class pimp, what does this job entail?"

"I call up, make the reservation, and any special requests. We go to dinner. I take them and wait for them until they're ready to leave."

"What do you do while you're waiting?" He flinched, and I realized my question had an accusatory tone and not by accident.

"I don't do anything, but sit in the waiting area drinking coffee and checking my watch."

"Well, if you hate it so much, then quit." Seemed like a simple solution to me.

He crossed his arms as if he was brandishing a shield. "With the exception of that I like the real part of my job, I couldn't make this kind of money doing this job anywhere else. Those nice little bonuses I get are in cash. Tax-free cash. Do you think I can afford a three hundred and fifty thousand dollar condo making eighty thousand dollars a year? Or my car, or everything else? I don't have any of this without this job."

Bile kept rising and rising, and I fought to keep from vomiting. "You're not a high class pimp. You're a fuckin' prostitute."

He stomped to the kitchen, jerked open the

refrigerator door, popped open a bottle of beer, and downed half in one breath. "You're right. I am. So, in order to keep any remaining respect you have for me, I'll go in, quit my job, and look for something else." He finished the beer. I waited for shattered glass and a bloody hand after the loud clank on the granite reverberated through the room.

"You better go find some boxes because we'll be moving out of here."

A dangerous tension crackled in the air. Not since the catalyst that stopped our original Dom/sub relationship, had we come so close to disintegrating. My hands splayed across my mouth in disbelief. I never thought anything could tear us apart again. We were dangling by unraveling threads. "Jordan, we need to go back to why we were havin' this conversation in the first place. Now's not the time to make life changes."

I had to stop to compose myself or I'd collapse in tears. "Your alibi. Whether I like what it is or not, you still have an alibi. This will go away, and then we can decide if we need to make any changes."

He swallowed hard and a sadness veiled across his face. "I don't."

I was drowning in confusion. "Did we not have a whole argument about where you were? You have an alibi. Whoever you were with or whoever saw you can vouch for you."

"They can't. I can't ask someone for whom anonymity is a must to say where they were, and they were with me. I can't violate that trust."

I gripped my hair so tight with my hand, one more squeeze would hail half of the right side of my hair sliding through my fingers. "Are you fucking kidding me? There's a possibility of you being accused of murder, and you have a legitimate alibi you won't use because of some fucked up loyalty?"

Enough. My ears, my brain, my body…and my heart struggled to process what he was saying. He chose them over us. He chose his job over me. I whipped around to seek refuge on our balcony. I didn't trust myself to walk out the door and return.

"Angel," he pleaded. "Come back here," he yelled.

Over my shoulder, I flipped him the bird. I had nothing else to offer. My heart burst leaving tiny shards scattered across the floor of a three hundred and fifty thousand dollar condo bought with fuck money.

"Don't call me that. She's dying, Jordan. You made your choice, and you're letting her die."

Chapter Twenty-Six
Jordan

I don't know what time Emma crawled into bed, but I do know I was awake. I'd never shut my eyes once except to wipe the water pooling in them. She slipped under the comforter where I sweltered but didn't bother to remove it.

Her back created a wall keeping me away, but as she flipped her hair from her face, the longest tendrils crashed on my bare chest. I froze, holding my breath waiting for her to say something, but instead a lingering sigh and a sniff made the darkness even darker.

Surreptitiously, I inserted two fingers into the curl. Last night, I anchored my hand in the mass extracting a moan so low and deep, I almost shot my wad right then. And now, I teetered on the edge of losing everything, the one who I loved more than life itself.

A darky silky and twisted rope hung over an impervious wall of contempt. I seized maybe the only opportunity I had left and rolled on my side. I draped my arm across her waist. Her body stiffened, but she didn't pull away from me. At least one tiny ember of hope flickered.

****

Ready to leave for work and needing to leave for work, but yet I couldn't stop myself from being a voyeur in my own bedroom. Her exposed arm shined as the canvas for my marks. They would fade in a few days, but I remembered sketching each one—some deeper and harder than others to change her soft moans to cries of praising the heavens in a not so heavenly manor. I never stopped until my masterpiece of her ravishment was complete.

Now, I'd destroyed our unforgettable weekend and possibly our future with a lie.

I wasn't angry at her words nor her lack of understanding why I couldn't ask my clients that night for their help. They were such masterful liars. Even if subpoenaed the two could convince everyone they were in bed asleep after our dinner like good little boys should be. The truth would backfire and make me look guilty.

Somewhere in the night, we broke apart and retreated to opposite sides of the bed. When I woke, I wanted to wrap myself around her body and wish her heart could forgive me, but I was afraid. Instead, I found a fraction of solace in a shower so hot my skin glowed red.

Picking up my suit jacket from the chair in the corner, I examined each sleeve for telltale lint, but in actuality I was stalling—questioning the rationale of waking her with the information I was leaving for the day. I chose a coward's way out. Brushing her hair from her face, I settled a light kiss on her cheek. She stirred, but didn't wake—or at least she pretended not to wake.

Once at work, I busied myself with the seventy-five things on my to-do list. Still, thoughts of last night blew through my mind, killing my focus in a hail of angry word bullets.

"Jordan?"

Mr. Levendar's voice startled me. "Yes. Come in."

"Are you okay?" He approached my desk with a hesitancy like I had a contagious disease.

"Sure. Why do you ask?"

"You were sitting at your desk with your hands buried on each side of your head like you had a migraine."

"Too many irons in the fire I suppose."

"That's kind of your specialty, now isn't it?" Levendar chuckled, swept the chair aside and plopped himself down like he owned the place…which he did.

Crossed legs and arms projected the extent of his daunting nature. He'd always been good to me, but when the king made any stick of furniture his throne, the answer was yes no matter what.

"Harry Luescher called me last night."

Why would he do that?

I probably set myself up for getting my dick chopped off, but I wasn't thrilled about that information. "Isn't there a thing…client, attorney privilege?"

I can't say he gave me the evil-eye, but one arched eyebrow and a slight tilt of his head clearly meant *No*.

"Luescher is the best. He can be an asshole to the nth degree, but he's the best. You might need his skills. I hope not, but nonetheless be prepared."

When the CEO/owner of your place of employment absorbs all the oxygen from the room in one deep breath and clasps his hands behind his head, you are about to have a *come to Jesus moment.*

"I hope not either, but I did get the impression it wasn't his first rodeo."

"I know you didn't do this, but I also know the utmost importance of confidentiality. If unflattering information about one of our whale clients were to come to light, this whole company *and* its employees would be at risk of losing everything."

A manifestation of cold reality rose to the surface of his face, frightening and steadfast.

What else could I say? "I completely understand, sir. You won't have any worries."

"Glad we're on the same page. If it comes to a head, let Luescher do his job."

"I will."

As he rose from the chair, his large frame exuded an intimidation vibe I'd never witnessed, and there was no way in hell I'd betray him.

"We both have work to do." Before he exited my office, he turned. "Jordan, I do greatly appreciate everything you do."

Yeah, well, my wife doesn't. Not one bit.

I never left my office the rest of the morning. I even had my admin order lunch out. Normally, if I were having a bad day, I'd call Angel and ask her to meet me for lunch. I wasn't too sure she'd answer the phone. Can't say I blamed her.

My admin burst through the door. "Mr. Caldera. That guy is back. The cop. He's coming down the hall.

Fuck. Fuck. Fuck.

I peeked out the door and a sudden terror began to suffocate me. He was so close, I didn't have time to call Angel.

"Mr. Caldera. I have a warrant for your arrest. You have the right to…"

I heard nothing else as one pulled my hands behind

my back and the cold feel of handcuffs directed my immediate future. Everything blurred. A dizziness descended on my brain, and I no longer had any feeling anywhere in my body except extreme despondence.

An office crowd gathered to watch my parade of shame.

One face stood out clear to me. Cameron Terry looked genuinely stricken as I passed by him.

Chapter Twenty-Seven
Angel

When I woke that morning, I had trouble distinguishing if what happened last night was a nightmare or had Jordan confessed to taking men to secret sex clubs. I rolled over splaying my hand over Jordan's side of the bed. The sheets were cold, but rumpled. Then I remembered a hesitant arm around my waist last night. Yes indeed, last night happened.

I had a full day's work ahead of me but not the strength to open a document. I needed a distraction. Grabbing my phone from the nightstand, I noticed the screen void of message notifications. Opening the window for texting, I entered SA and Sabrina's name popped up on the receiver line.

—You want to come over today. I'm having bad day, and you're leaving soon.—

Within seconds, I had my answer. *—On my way.—*

The beauty of a lifelong friendship is the free pass on hygiene. I didn't need to shower. My pajamas could remain winkled and smelly without judgment.

Sabrina made her own coffee. Apparently, Jordan left without having any breakfast. I slathered a bagel half overflowing and dripping with strawberry cream cheese, poured a glass of milk, and grabbed a banana before joining her at the bar counter.

"So, are you packed and ready to move to

Chicagoland?"

"Sort of. I still have this bug niggling at the back of my head questioning the level of bad idea this is."

"Well, smack the little fuck and flick it from your mind. I know you two've not known each other very long, but when it's right it is."

A dreamy, fairytale grin expanded across her face. She sparkled—reminding me of me a few years ago. My sparkle dulled last night with a shard of confession.

"Stop playing games and tell me what's wrong. You keep driving the conversation back to me and Cameron. And as much as I'm into him, I know that's not why I'm here. So, stop circumventing the situation and tell me."

Before I began to explain, babblings between sobs claimed my voice. She waited patiently until I stopped the waterworks and returned to coherency. "Jordan confessed to me last night that sometimes when he takes clients out, they go to this underground sex club."

Her mouth dropped so wide, you could've inserted a fist. Cameron had kept her in the dark as well. Jordan was right about one thing, I shouldn't tell her. That was Cameron's admission to make.

"I'm sure he doesn't…partake. Right?"

"He said he doesn't. I believe him, but the whole thing crushes me. I don't understand how a man who's married or has a significant other thinks doing that is okay, and that Jordan thinks it's okay because his boss wants him to—even if he gives him a nice bonus. It's not. I guess the place is good at being under the radar. I've never heard of Heaven's Gate Yacht Club."

Sabrina's eyes peered over the mug of steaming coffee. "So are you mad because he goes or are you mad because he didn't tell you?"

"I, uh." Last night I thought angry covered all the bases. How dare she make me decide?

"Let me put it this way. If he had told you would you still be angry?"

"Yes, but…maybe not quite at the same level."

"I'm well aware you have ton loads more relationship experience than I do. I mean look at me. I fell for the first guy who ever tied me up."

I think I snotted into my bagel. "God, I love you."

"Anyway, how important will this argument be in five years, ten years, or if one of you is in a hospital bed with cancer?"

"It won't mean shit." I knew in my heart Jordan was a good person caught up in an employment hard place. Would I've done the same thing? I couldn't claim to be any farther along the ethics line than the average person. Would I've told him? I couldn't answer.

I scraped the damaged side of the bagel free of possible contamination but continued to munch the chewy bread. My phone vibrated, then started ringing. Probably Jordan calling. The screen read Cameron.

I snatched up my phone and glanced at Sabrina. "Why would Cameron be calling me? Is your phone on?"

"Yeah."

"Hi, Cameron. Bri's here if you're looking for her."

Silence.

"Cameron?"

"Emma, the police just left the office. Jordan's been arrested."

Chapter Twenty-Eight
Angel

I don't remember falling. You never hit bottom in your dreams. Swirls of yellow and gray—the colors in my kitchen zigzagged across my vision in a blur. This was a dream—no, a nightmare. I clawed at my skin, raking my nails from ear to jaw.

Again and again, I dug into my skin, but nothing cut through the numbness. I needed to wake up, but I couldn't.

A woman's voice in the distance rang tinny and garbled in my ear but kept saying the same thing over and over. "Stop. Stop it." I realized the voice belonged to Bri, but where was she? I couldn't see her. Something gripped my shoulders like a vise, keeping me from moving. I struggled, wrenching my arms from the unknown snare, and pure adrenaline pumped through my veins giving me the strength to break from the trap. I scrambled to my feet, but kept stumbling.

Air. My body demanded air. Through the fuzzy tunnel in my head, I saw the glass doors leading to our balcony. Again Bri's voice echoed in the distance, "Jaynie, stop," but I didn't listen. If I couldn't get outside, I'd suffocate.

Grabbing the brass handle on the French doors to our balcony, I lifted the knob and thrust the door open. The air I craved, hit my face with the blast of a furnace.

I imposed a death grip on the metal railing, rested my forehead on top, while my lungs heaved, frantic for oxygen.

Time passes at its own pace when you're terrified. I don't know how long I sagged on the railing, but I do remember warm masculine arms hugging my shaky shoulders. Jordan was waking me up from this hideous dream.

Instead, I smelled a woodsy scent—Cameron

"Emma, I got you. Let me help you." The reassuring words belonged not to my husband, but his sworn enemy.

Giving in to my consciousness, I now knew my nightmare existed outside of my head. In one movement I turned into Cameron's chest and sobbed. "This is my fault, all my fault." The strength and warmth of his body hugging mine did nothing to ease my anguish.

His arms tightened. "No, it's not your fault."

I didn't feel better because none of this would have happened if not for me.

"Look at me."

I refused. As long as I stayed plastered to his chest, I didn't have to acknowledge how this all came to be.

Cameron unhooked my arms from his waist and forced me away from him. He gripped my chin with constraint, giving no choice but to meet him eye for eye—the intensity of his clutch in direct contrast to the calming embrace only seconds ago.

"This is *not* your fault. It's *not* Jordan's fault. This is a bullshit call by the cops. But you, you can't be this way." He squeezed harder. "Shit could get a whole lot worse, and you have to be strong. You cannot fall apart because Jordan needs you."

I nodded as best I could with his death grip on my chin. "Will you take me down there?"

"Yes, we will." Bri rested one hand on Cameron's shoulder and one on mine.

Whereas, I was confident I was covered in blotchy red, Bri appeared even paler than her normal skin tone. She was as scared as I was.

I flashed back to the conversation I had with him the first time I met Cameron at the fancy party. The last thing he said to me after he handed me his card and before Jordan stormed in was "you might need to call me sometime."

Never did I imagine the reason I needed Cameron now was that the police believed my husband had murdered someone. The man I'd rarely seen angry. The man who had the kindest soul I'd ever known. I didn't care what Cameron said, I was responsible.

With Cameron's arm around my shoulder and Bri's around my waist, they guided me through the door into the cool air of my living room. Whether inside of me or out, every part of my anatomy hummed with numbness.

"Go wash your face, put on some clothes, and we can go," Cameron said. "Have you called the attorney?"

In the selfish meltdown of my world, I only thought about what'd happened and not what to do. "No, I didn't. His number's in my phone, Harry Luescher. Would you call?"

"Sure."

Cameron retrieved my phone from the kitchen floor, while I made my way to the bathroom. So, this was what a zombie felt like—dead on the inside, but still walking.

After a hot and abrasive scrubbing, I dried my face and caught a glimpse in the mirror. No amount of makeup could hide my despair. As I gathered my hair into a ponytail, I nearly doubled over from the vicious wave of nausea sweeping through my stomach. I dropped to my knees seconds before vomiting into the toilet. When I raised my head to wipe my mouth, my eyes swam with dizziness and then I retched again.

You cannot fall apart; Jordan needs you.

Chapter Twenty-Nine
Jordan

Booked, fingerprinted, mugshot. I watched a horror movie in 3-D. Only problem was, I was the star, the monster they hunted and cornered. How did this all go so wrong?

After the first question Rausch asked me while in the interrogation room, I knew I was in trouble. He didn't wait for an answer. The questions were leading, and rapid fired one after the other. I said nothing until I heard a pause in his inquisition.

"I won't say anything until my lawyer is with me."

No more questions until Luescher arrived.

The maddening silence made hours out of minutes. Someone swabbed my cheek for a DNA sample. When they passed the law requiring everyone arrested for a crime to give a sample, the decision to me was right and fair. At the time, I never imagined a part of me would forever be in a database.

Never thought about how I'd behave or feel if I was ever arrested. Never thought I would be. My whole criminal history amounted to the cops making me dump the contents of a case of beer when I was sixteen years old. I was more concerned about watching my money run down the street than anything else.

Angel was furious with me for not telling her what I'd been doing, but even more so when I said I wouldn't divulge who was with me. There was no point. In their world, I was nobody but the cruise director on their ship of iniquity—one they'd all deny ever knowing existed. My biggest concern had always been what would I do when one of them had a fucking heart attack in the club? I'd devised a contingency plan for old fucks dropping dead but not one for me being accused of murder.

Sometime between five minutes and a perceived fifteen hours, Harry Luescher walked into the room looking every bit as fresh pressed as I was wrinkled and crushed.

"Jordan, I would ask how you're doing, but in a fucked up situation like this, the answer is obvious."

"What happens now? Can I call my wife?"

He remained standing. I had the feeling our meeting would be short and not end on a positive note. "They can hold you for seventy-two hours. At that time, you'll either be charged or released—don't expect the latter. There'll be a court appearance when you can enter your plea. Unfortunately you won't be able to talk to your wife until after you're moved."

"Moved?"

"To the jail."

"Until bail is set, right?"

His jaw tightened and a grim line formed across his mouth. "I'm sorry to tell you, the state of Indiana does not allow bail for anyone charged with murder."

Chapter Thirty
Angel

"No, that can't be true." I'd been studying our bank accounts when Mr. Luescher informed me. His cocked eyebrow challenged me.

"I'm sorry. I wasn't trying to argue the law with you. I can't believe this is happening. I see all the time about the accused being out on bail...I mean crazy amounts sometimes, but still..."

"Not in this state, unfortunately."

"I need to see him. I need to see he's okay." My teeth chattered, and I clenched my fists to stop my trembling hands.

"Mrs. Caldera, you can't do that either."

My fear gave birth to fury. "Whatever became of innocent until proven guilty? Jordan's never done anything. It's not fair."

A gentle squeeze caught my attention. I glanced and noted Cameron's hand resting on my shoulder as Luescher spoke "Emma, there's nothing—"

I jerked free. Anger, fear, and disbelief mixed a deadly recipe of nausea churning in my gut. My head burned with the heat, and sweat from my head ran a path down the back of my neck. My scalped itched like I was infested with fleas. "What good are you if you can't do anything for him? He shouldn't be there."

"Jaynie, please." Bri's voice shook, and I realized

the incivility of my words. One by one tears raced across my cheeks. "I'm sorry. I didn't mean. I'm very sorry, Mr. Luescher."

For the first time since we met, I watched a hint of empathy dawn across his face. "I understand. This is a new, unknown, and extremely frightening circumstance. Pretty high on the stress level. Once there is a court appearance and charges made, he will be given a more—I don't want to say permanent—but rather a settled situation. At that point, arrangements can be made for contact. Until then, you can write a letter, I can give it to him. I'm sure he'd appreciate it. But make no references to what has happened. Nothing is private in jail."

My voice caught in my throat. I nodded slightly. My grip on reality slipped finger by finger from the icy ledge. If Cameron hadn't grabbed my waist, I would have collapsed on the concrete floor. The last words Jordan and I shared came out of anger.

They drove me home, opened my door, and walked my numb body to the sofa. Bri brought me tea, but a few minutes later I heard Cameron and her whispering in the kitchen.

"Whatever you guys are talking about please tell me." I called without glancing their way, but rather I stared into my tea waiting to wake up from this nightmare.

I set the mug on the floor and joined them. Whether they wanted me or not, I was crashing this meeting.

"You need to tell Jordan's parents before this hits the news," Cameron said.

The tingling surging down my legs cut my veins

with razor-sharp shards of dawning. Jordan's parents were fun loving and very much like the son they raised. This news would devastate them as much as it had me.

"You want me to call them?" Cameron asked.

"Do you know them?"

"Not at all. They're as off limits as you are, but this'll be a very difficult call."

Understatement of a lifetime.

"I'll do it. I'm not sure what to say though. They know nothing of what's been going on. Well, actually, they know nothing about our other life."

Bri handed me my phone. I stared at the piece, which was so often another appendage to my body. My life in a three by six box of electronics. How many times had I giggled and turned red at Jordan's texts—or got so horny I had to get myself off that very minute and *suffer* his discipline when he'd told me not to. I touched the photo icon. Five hundred and thirty six glimpses of our life. Not every photo was of one of us, but every photo meant something to our lives.

I scrolled through a few photos until I noticed drops of water on my screen. Tears. One huge sniff and two deep breaths later, I'd recovered enough I thought to place two very terrifying phone calls—one to Jordan's parents and one to my dad.

Anthony Caldera answered on the second ring. I'd secretly hoped for a voicemail. Machines had no emotion and no judgment.

"Emma, hello. Glad you called. Jenny wanted me to call Jordan later to see if the two of you wanted to try out the new Cajun place down the road from us. Saturday maybe?"

Saturday. A few days and maybe a lifetime away.

"Um, Anthony, I have something…"

I did the only thing I could do. "Jordan's been arrested." I blurted into the phone.

"What? Say that again?" Yeah. I couldn't believe those words either.

"The police went to Jordan's office…and they took him to jail."

"What in the hell for?" I know he was agitated I'd said so little, but the words were a heavy black tar on my tongue sticking at the tip, and I tried to ply them away one by one.

"There was a woman, and she wrote this thing, and she wasn't supposed to say who we were, but she was going to. We tried to stop her, but she wasn't going to listen. The police found her body, and they think Jordan did it."

"Emma, you're not making sense. Tell me again." In the background, I heard Jenny. "Anthony what's going on, what's happened. Is it one of the kids?"

I knew I didn't make sense. None of this made sense. How could the police assume? "I'm sorry. I don't know what to say." The itchy sensation of streams of sweat trickling down my spine made me want to strip my clothes off. At that moment, everything seemed too tight. Even the little thin cord of my collar choked the breath from me, but it wasn't for me to remove.

Jordan secured those rights long ago.

I tried again to find the right words. My brain was in one of the glass tanks that blew money from the bottom. Every word in frenzied flight avoided my attempts to snag what I needed to say. "A few months ago, I gave an interview to a reporter. Everything was supposed to be secret. She didn't know who we really were, but she found out. I did the interview with the promise no one would ever know our identities." While what I was saying was correct, there's was no way Jordan's dad would understand. I had no choice but to tell him. "The article was about people who live a different life, and in our case, our story was about BDSM." There, I'd said it.

Other than Jessica Forner, the single other person I'd ever told about Jordan and my life was Bri, and now the third person was my father-in-law."

"I'm sorry, what?"

"Anthony, this woman was going to expose what we do by using our names. We tried to talk her out of doing it. I mean she promised. Someone killed her, and the police believe Jordan killed her."

"Oh my God. Oh my God. Jenny." His voice trailed off in the distance, but I kept hearing Oh my God, Oh my God—first Anthony and then Jenny, but Jenny's was more of a scream. I didn't know what to do. How devastating to hear your son's been arrested for murder, but equally as horrific when their son is the love of your life, and you know, you know with all your heart he didn't do it.

The longer I waited for someone to come back on the phone, the worse the pain and nausea grew in my stomach. We were well into the afternoon and I'd had nothing to eat but a portion of a bagel. Even such a small amount of food was…I could wait no more. I threw the phone and rushed to the bathroom—bumping into the sofa table, tripping over shoes and smacking the corner of the doorway leading to the bathroom. I ripped open the toilet lid seconds before violent waves of retching claimed me.

From the corner of my eye, I saw Bri gathering my hair behind my head. After a few more retches, I collapsed against the cold porcelain and welcomed the cooling tingle against my fiery cheek. A raw, bleeding pain furrowed through my insides—stripping away my sanity. My one decision had set my world to crumble.

Bri knelt beside me, placing her hands on my shoulders. "I know this is the wrong thing to say, but are you okay? I know you're not. None of us are, but what I mean is do we need to go to a med clinic or something?"

With the back of my hand, I wiped any residue from my mouth. "No, I... The more I talked to Jordan's dad, the worse it got. I'll be okay." I rested on my haunches and glanced through the doorway. I saw Cameron talking on my phone. Bri helped me to my feet, and we made our way to his side on uneasy steps as I swayed from the lightheadedness and the surreal images of a real-life nightmare.

"Yes, sir. I think that would be a good thing." Cameron said into the phone.

He ended the call and handed me my phone. "They're coming over to be with you and, uh, talk."

Chapter Thirty-One
Jordan

"Caldera, you have a visitor."

The jail officer's voice startled me from somewhere between dozing and shock. He didn't say "your lawyer's here." Luescher had left a few hours ago. They told me I could have no visitors for seventy-two hours. Hell, seventy-two hours could have passed already. From the strip search to the constant light in the cell, my recall of time passage bordered on non-existent. I hadn't eaten since the morning of the arrest. It's not like they didn't offer meals, I couldn't stomach anything. That and the fact what I'd seen of the food left me no appetite.

I had no choice but to give a DNA sample. The scratches on my forearm had scabbed over, but their visibility reminded me of my disastrous meeting with Jessica. I should have left things alone. Sure, the possibility of her publishing that story and outing us was pretty much a given. Considering what had happened, I'd take door number one in a heartbeat now.

The officer escorted me to the visiting area. Well, television and movies got that right. The set up and nonexistent décor resembled everything I'd ever watched in a movie. When I sat down on the metal folding chair in the booth-like cubicle, on the other side sat Mr. Levendar.

With hesitancy, I sat down. The old chair rattled under my weight as the legs scraped the floor. I picked up the phone receiver, but couldn't decide what to say. Why was he here? But the better question teetered on the edge of my tongue.

"Mr. Levendar, how did you get here? I didn't think I could have any visitors yet."

My boss sat directly across from me but miles away. His eyebrows cocked and a slight smile grazed his face. "It pays at times to know certain people…or should I say know certain people who are willing to bend the rules for certain people."

The smile made a rapid exit replaced by a stone exterior. "I know this is difficult and unequivocally unwarranted. I want to re-iterate what we talked about before. This situation will receive a lot of press, and I can't have my company dragged through the mud because you're tied to it. I'll have to distance myself and the company from this. I'm sorry. I'm most appreciative of what you do for our clients, but I must be assured they will not be jeopardized."

I detected the briefest moment of remorse when he shifted his focus from me to the gray Formica table in front of him.

He hadn't needed to make an appearance. I already understood exactly what couldn't be said. No one would substantiate my whereabouts anyway. I knew in their own minds they believed they had way more to lose, and I was nothing to them. I was nothing to those rich assholes.

A sad reconciliation extracted the little bit of energy I had remaining, and I wasn't sure my legs would hold me to walk away from here. "I understand completely, Mr. Levendar. You won't need to visit me again."

I removed the receiver from my ear, but before I could replace it on the wall, I heard Mr. Levendar say, "Luescher is the best. He's the best."

I nodded, but had nothing left to say. I had to put all my faith into a lawyer I couldn't afford without the support of an employer who could make this all go away. My wife believed she was to blame, but Angel wasn't. My absoluteness in being the hero, the one who saved the day, the one who had a solution to every problem had to accept culpability for this clusterfuck.

Then a thought slapped me upside the head.

My parents.

I'd been so otherwise consumed, I hadn't thought about my parents. Had Angel told them? God, I hated she would be the one who illuminated them on their son's secret needs. What would they say or how would they feel? Angel, who'd had a difficult enough time coming to grips with her desires, would have to explain the whole story. I could see my mom's face paling before glowing with the red of embarrassment. With his systematic approach to everything in life, my dad would have Angel create a timeline of events to find a nonexistent loophole.

Dad's landscaping business didn't carry the family name so customers might not connect Sunrise Landscaping to me. Mom however, was a different story. She had lots of public contact being the head librarian for Sutter Township Library. She shouldn't have to suffer that kind of public humiliation.

At least my sister Lessi understood the kink life. She was deeper into the life than I was. She also understood the need for anonymity. Maybe Lessi could help mitigate the blow, but by doing so, she'd out herself and it was unfair of me to even hope so.

What I'd really wanted was a hug from my Angel. The possibility existed only in my dreams I'd ever hold her again.

Chapter Thirty-Two
Angel

When the doorbell rang, I knew my dad stood on the other side. He lived much closer to us than Jordan's parents. Cameron had called him after he'd spoken to Anthony.

Gary Samuelson, my dad, had deep red hair that now blended with strands of gray at his temples with a few renegade wisps in the front. I knew why my mom first fell for him. Even at fifty-nine, he was a handsome man.

I remembered little about my mom, but Dad said I kept her alive. In photos of her, the woman could have been me and no one would know the difference. We looked identical, but also Dad said we had the same personality. Lord help him there. I knew I was a challenge growing up.

My dad had been both parents. He came to every school open house and teacher's conference. He took time off for class field trips. He drove to every single softball game I ever played. He learned to tame my wild hair, and he was the one who explained my period. He was my provider and my protector. At that moment, all I wanted to do was be daddy's little girl again and have him hug me and tell me everything would be all right.

Before I let him step inside, I threw my arms

around his neck and sobbed. "Oh, Dad this is such a nightmare. I don't know what to do."

I must have stood on his feet because he walked me into our living room while still hugging me. The story was bad enough to have to explain to Jordan's parents, but my own father…? I feared he would be angry, shocked, or the worst of all…disappointed in me.

"Tell me what's going on, and we'll work it out. We'll take care of it."

I released my grip only enough to look into his eyes. "Dad, you can't fix this."

Sabrina and Cameron faded into the background while I explained everything. And I mean not the details, but I had to reintroduce his daughter to him.

"Not exactly something I thought I'd ever hear, but if you and Jordan are happy, who am I to judge? You're not hurting anyone." He jerked his head toward the kitchen where Sabrina and Cameron were drinking coffee. "They know?"

I nodded. "They know. They uh, uh, indulge as well."

His eyes grew wide, and I could tell he was trying not to laugh. "Little Miss Pure as the Driven Snow? Her mother always thought you were a bad influence. I think her mother's a self-righteous ass wipe."

"Dad." Somehow, we'd gotten off track, but he made me smile with his spot-on description.

"Sorry. What can I do? Do you have a lawyer?"

"Yes. His name is Harry Luescher."

"Any good?"

"Jordan's boss recommended him. So, I assume so."

"Have they set bail?"

My heart dropped remembering the piece of information making everything ten times worse. "I found out there's no bail allowed in the state of Indiana when charged with murder."

"Well that's bullshit. What happened to innocent until proven guilty?"

Yeah. What happened?

The dinging of the doorbell sent the rocks tumbling in my stomach. Jordan's parents. I caught my dad's sympathetic expression. My dad, the guy I thought could do anything, was as helpless as I was. "That's Jordan's mom and dad, I'm sure."

"I'll get it." Sabrina hurried to the door instead of Cameron. They'd met her at our wedding, but Cameron was a complete stranger, other than the brief words they exchanged while I was puking my guts out.

Jenny was first through the door. Her red-rimmed eyes told me she'd cried the whole way over here. Anthony was right on her heels, followed by Jordan's sister Alessia. She was Jordan with boobs, almost as tall and absolutely stunning.

I stood to greet them, and Jenny hugged me so hard, I lost my breath. Anthony followed and what little resolve I'd gained talking with my dad washed away in one touch.

"This is such a shock," Anthony said. "Emma, can you give us more details? What can we do to help Jordan?"

With my dad clutching my hand, I went into auto pilot mode giving details. I heard my voice, but I wasn't there. Some entity had invaded my body—an entity with a matter-of-fact attitude, stone emotions, and perfect diction. I'd never seen her before, but I hated her and loved her at the same time. I needed her and not me.

I filled the air with everything the lawyer had told me right down to the devastating minutia of my home state's stand on bail. My dad and I weren't alone in the unaware department. I'd have sold everything we owned to get Jordan home.

Anthony slumped in disappointment and Jenny started crying again. "I'd already contacted the bank about withdrawing a large amount," he said.

Jenny asked me about the kink. *Why* seemed to be her biggest concern, followed by a *where did we go wrong* soliloquy.

"Was it the scouts?" she asked.

"What're you talking about?" Anthony couldn't hide his confusion.

"When Jordan was young he was a scout."

"What the hell has that got to do with anything?"

Jenny let out an exasperated sigh. "Don't you remember, Jordan won all those awards in knot tying?"

If the situation hadn't been so dire, I'd have found her comment hilarious.

"Mom," Alessia broke in, "a knot tying award has nothing to do with why Jordan's the way he is."

Jenny straightened with an indignant posture. "Lessie, you don't know that."

Alsessia stared at the ceiling before closing her eyes, and I knew what was about to come. Could his parents take any more disclosures today?

"Mom, I know because the same womb isn't the only thing Jordan and I share."

This time, Jenny's expression contorted with

confusion, but Anthony seemed to make the connection instantly. Whisky may have been the only solution for today.

"I participate in the lifestyle too," Alessia said.

Jenny's startled reaction made her glances dart around the condo like a frightened sparrow. "Lifestyle? What is this lifestyle? Like porn? You do porn?"

Lessie's fists curled and uncurled, and I know she began mentally counting. "Mom, this isn't really the time. We're here for Jordan. All I'll say now is Jordan and Emma, and I have made different choices for expressing our sexuality, and we're completely normal people."

Jenny gave both Lessie and me a hesitant smile. "You're right, honey. This is something we can discuss…or not discuss at another time. I'm terrified. I know Jordan wouldn't ever hurt anyone."

We moved to the dining room table and talked about nothing. Someone ordered a pizza that remained untouched. The smell of the meat and cheese made me nauseous. For hours we stared at one another, made the most inane chitchat about the weather, the upcoming football season, and the horrible construction delays on the highway. But every few minutes or so we paused for a brief few seconds and then one of us would wonder if Jordan was okay or when we could see him.

We strayed from topic to topic in order to keep the what-ifs at bay, but knew we had to hold in reverence the severity of the situation—Jordan's current safety as well as his future.

Innocent people didn't go to prison.

Yes, they did.

Hours passed of hearing stories of Jordan and

Lessi's childhood intermittingly mixed with "when would Luescher call with news?" Late in the evening, Anthony announced as much as he hated to leave me, they should go home and prepare for comments and phone calls he knew would come their way.

All three of them hugged me good-bye with the promise to come back tomorrow. My dad offered to stay the night, but I said he didn't need to. Bri and Cameron also offered, and when it whittled down to Bri alone, I still said no. I loved them and needed their support, but more than anything, I needed the darkness and silence and the scent of my husband on our sheets. Only then could I release the growing force of anguish piercing my heart and the very soul of my being.

Chapter Thirty-Three
Angel

Days passed, and formal charges of murder were filed against Jordan. He was established as an official inmate of the county jail. According to Luescher, we could be waiting months for the trial to start.

Months.

Since we'd gotten married, the number of days Jordan and I spent apart were few. Every morning when I woke up, I saw his face, embraced his warmth, and reveled in the thought we were one life. But those days had vanished, and little by little, even his presence in my sheets faded.

I dug his dirty clothes from the laundry hamper. I'd refused to wash them, and when Bri almost threw them in the washer, I went psycho on her. I apologized in tears, knowing she was trying to help me, but I slept with his clothes every night, wrapping myself in his dress shirts and tucking those stupid college T-shirts around me in the bed. That's all I had left of him.

Bri nagged and nagged me to eat, but even when I tried, everything came up. Despite the lack of food, I wasn't hungry but exhausted.

She came by one last time before she and Cameron moved to Chicago. She'd offered to stay until everything was over, but I couldn't ask so much of her. She and Cameron were beginning their own future, and she deserved her own happiness. Bri was far from Cameron's usual type, but I know he loved her. Three hours and an interstate separated Indianapolis and Chicago. We'd have the weekends.

We'd have the weekends. Sure.

I tried to eat an egg, but wound up in the bathroom heaving away again. When Bri let herself in, she found me brushing my teeth. With a mouthful of toothpaste, I nose pointed to the plastic grocery bag she carried.

"Wha u guot inwa bag?" I mumbled.

"For you," she said. She set the bag on the sink. "I know this is the most stressful thing that can happen to a person, but I think something else is going on with you being sick all the time."

She slipped her hand in the bag, and opened her palm to me. Resting in her hand sat a pregnancy test.

Pregnancy test. Holy fuck, no, I couldn't be pregnant. "There's no way I could be pregnant."

"And you're absolutely positive about that. So, you've had a recent period?"

I never gave pregnancy much thought. With the shot, I didn't even have periods. I believed it could be at least a few months before I could be pregnant. Probably should have talked to my doctor about the process and plausibility. "I haven't had a period in a long time because of the birth control I was on. So, no, I've not had a period, but I don't think it unusual."

She shoved the test toward me.

"Bri, I'm not pregnant. I'm major stressed. I finally get to see Jordan today."

She shoved again. "Then he needs to know if you are."

"Fine. I'll pee on the stick."

Chapter Thirty-Four
Angel

"Are you going to vomit again?"

I barely heard her words as I stared open-mouthed at the little plus sign.

"Jaynie?"

No, no, no.

This couldn't have happened. And I thought things couldn't have gotten worse.

"Jaynie!"

"What? What? What fucking what?"

Not even fazed by my rude explosion. "What does it say?"

I handed her my future. "I'm pregnant."

She grabbed me, hugging me tight. "I'm so happy for you."

I'm sure my stiffened body caused her to release me.

"This is what you wanted. We talked and you said you couldn't wait to see Jordan holding your…"

She clamped her mouth shut.

My plan. Planning wasn't my forte, but when I didn't redo my birth control, I'd already started, with a notebook and everything, from the baby elephant décor in the baby's room, to the six hundred and seventy-five pictures on my phone of Jordan being a dad. What's that quote about making a plan is a way to make God laugh?

She latched onto my stiff shoulders, and I struggled to find the strength to stay on my feet. "Look. Don't think of this as bad timing. Granted it's not the best, but this is good thing. Jordan'll be happy. He will. He needs something good to hold onto, and like you, and this baby is what you need." Her grip tightened, and her nails dug into my skin. "You need a reason to take care of yourself."

The nausea I'd endured earlier was nothing compared to the concrete settling in my stomach. When I woke up, the excitement about getting to see my husband rippled through my body, but then, I had to determine whether to tell him I was pregnant or wait.

****

While Jordan's family wanted to see him too, the jail rules stated only one of us could go. He was allowed a video visit at another time, and the number of people allowed for that type of visit was not restricted.

As I walked to the jail from the parking garage, Harry Luescher accompanied me, but he would remain in a waiting area. He versed me on what not to say. Conversations weren't private. I wished he had told me what to say. Contrary to what some people believed, I'd never been arrested or even been near the inside of a jail.

Sitting in the metal chair, my heart pounded through my chest, and the icy cold metal numbed my ass even through the jeans I wore. While I waited, I wondered what Jordan would look like, what I would say to him, and what would he say to me. The entire drive I practiced my brave face. My determination not to cry when I saw him zapped my energy. Now that I knew I was pregnant, I had no idea whether the pounding headache or churning nausea was physical or psychological.

When the door opened, I held my breath and the copper taste of blood spread across my tongue. I had clamped down on my lip to keep from reacting to his haggard appearance.

Since I'd known him, Jordan hadn't gone more than two days without shaving. Even with daily shaves, by the end of day, the scruff reappeared. Now, the beginning of a beard covered his pale face, but nothing could hide the dark circles under his eyes. The fear, the worry, the unknowing had all taken a toll on him.

He gave me a weak smile, and even that seemed to require a concentrated extraction of energy. A part of me wished I hadn't come, and I hated myself for the thought. This man who'd always been so strong and in control for me, needed me to be the same way. I didn't think I was up for the task. Up until a few weeks ago, my most significant challenge was choosing the lifestyle, but since his arrest, forcing myself out of bed was a close second.

What do you say in this situation? I had no idea.

"I never thought I'd see the day you had nothing to say," Jordan said through the receiver.

An overwhelming sadness draped over me. I couldn't bite hard enough to stop the tears escaping down my cheeks.

"Emma, don't. I'm all right. You don't have to say anything. I need to see you, your face, your everything."

I do have to say one thing.

"Are you really? You don't look all right. I mean

you shouldn't look okay. This is a nightmare, Jordan."

Still icy blue and beautiful, but his eyes told me the truth. He wasn't fine. He was a good man thrown in with people who'd actually committed crimes...real murderers. Anyone would be scared.

"Has your lawyer been here much?"

"A few times. He said we'll meet more when there is actually something new to talk about. He said he wanted to meet with you privately."

I had no clue whether a meeting with the lawyer was a bad thing, a good thing, or a formality. "I hope it's soon. I don't like not knowing anything."

"Me either."

Tell him.

"Jordan? I need..." My brain slammed the door on my news. Announcing a baby should be a happy moment between a husband and wife. It should also be a private one.

Time froze, but not in the way of our normal. We weren't seeing each other from across the room and telegraphing what would happen later. I wasn't bound to a bed unable to move as Jordan prepared to stalk and devour me. No, time froze because we both knew but were either unwilling or afraid this could be our new normal.

Justice didn't always prevail.

"Emma what is it?"

I closed my eyes and blurted. "I'm pregnant."

Nothing. I didn't even hear him breathing through the receiver. For the first time, I regretted not talking with him before I stopped my birth control. My practical and levelheaded husband would have had a very long and involved discussion about having a child right now. Big step, changes in our lives in every facet, very big decision…Things like that. I didn't want to have the discussion because the thing that drove me the craziest about Jordan was he wanted to talk about *everything.* Maybe, he had good reason. Even though at the cabin, he said he was okay with starting a family, I knew secretly not having the discussion probably had instigated a severe case of heartburn in him.

When I found enough courage to open my eyes, my fear vanished. Jordan was smiling—not his normal grand expression, but rather a slight upturn of his lips telling me he was pleased.

"You have to change your mind about having an alib—"

"Emma, stop."

His immediate shift from happy to angry shocked me. This was no longer he and I. We were having a baby. He had an alibi.

"Jordan you can make them testify. Make them tell the truth." His hand slammed against the glass, and I flinched.

"Stop. Just stop it. This doesn't' change anything. It's not gonna happen no matter what either of us wants."

How could he let it go? My skin burned, and I wondered if my cheeks were as red as the flaming burn I experienced. So what if Big Brother was listening. "So, you don't really care about seeing your child?

I followed his swallow all of the way down his neck. I regretted my words, but still I said nothing else and watched his own anger build.

"No, no I don't care…at all. Why would I?" Jordan blinked repeatedly and his eyes grew dark.

Through the receiver, his tone frightened me. "I'm perfectly fine with you raising our child alone or finding someone else to help. Yes, Emma, I'm okay with never seeing my child."

As moisture gathered in his eyes, he laid the receiver on the table and raked both hands through his hair before turning his eyes to the wall.

"Jordan, I'm sorry." Then I realized he couldn't hear me. I tapped on the glass and his grave stare broke my heart. I pleaded with my own eyes for him to pick up the phone.

His voice no longer angry, but melancholy. "I wish I could make you understand."

My simple breakfast of cereal threatened to come up, and I covered my mouth like that would stop the motion. "You're right. I don't really understand. I know I need to trust you, but I'm so scared. I'm so scared."

We said nothing else, but stared through the glass at each other silently expressing feelings, fears, love, and alarm until Jordan glanced over his shoulder at the guard.

Time was up.

Like I'd seen so many times in the movies, I placed my hand on the glass and Jordan followed. I know my imagination kicked in, but touching my husband's hand gave me a moment of calm.

"I love you," I said.

"I always love you, Angel...momma."

My heart skipped at his declaration. Someone would be calling me Mom. How did my own mom feel when I called for her? If I hadn't had my dad around when she died, what would have happened to me?

Chapter Thirty-Five
Jordan

A baby.

I wasn't expecting to hear those words. Luescher had told me and her as well, I'm sure, not to talk about anything related to the case. I shouldn't have been surprised she brought up my alibi. And I shouldn't have gotten angry. Nobody more than I wanted to give the police the names of the two men with me that night. With no paper trail, I couldn't prove anything. My word against theirs and their words true or not had much more clout than mine.

The man who headed a family empire representing a wholesome family entertainment broadcast channel would never, ever frequent an underground sex club, would he? His son might, but not if the two of them were together on a trip to find a company who could best promote the values they believed in and practiced. Only people with low morals would let such depravity ever lay a finger on them.

Fuck me. They gave me a list of preferences so long, I had to work with the club's owner for weeks to make sure every item could be checked off by the end of the night. More than a few times, Mr. Levendar had *casually* mentioned how important this account was. Landing this whale meant millions of dollars coming back to us if they chose us to do their marketing. And the bonus. Yes, the hefty bonus I'd see for my efforts propelled me to ensure their visit was memorable.

They'd raved to Levendar about what I'd provided. While the club was secret, nothing about Heaven's Boat Yacht Club was sleazy and catered to the wealthy connoisseur of unconventional sex. And when people asked what they did on their visit, why, they went to the yacht club...in a landlocked city.

If someone asked for their timeline, I provided their perfect alibi. My company credit card slip for dinner was time stamped around eight thirty in the evening, and I even drove them back to their hotel to pick up something one of them had left in the room. Hotel staff could verify the two were there before nine that night. A nice neat little package to keep them from helping me.

A baby.

My baby. Our baby. Wow. Somehow, I'd thought the circumstances and setting would have been different. I'd always expected such news to be a private moment. Nothing in jail was private. After my first court appearance, I got a roommate and an audience for taking a shit.

I might have dozed but sleep...no. A light was always on, like summer in Alaska, but the scenery was traumatizing.

None of that mattered now. My wife was going to have a baby, and I could do nothing, but pray for a good outcome. I stared at the dirty white painted ceiling for hours, missing lunch in the process. No loss there. The white provided a screen where I projected the images of my life. Angel graced nearly every scene. Over and over again, she appeared. The night we first met, I'd spotted her long before she spilled the wine on me. Afterwards, she was all I could think about.

I always had to tell Angel to breathe. Truth was I had to tell my own self to breathe. When I watched and studied her body while she labored in her bonds, my lungs froze. She was beautiful and mine.

How long before I was witness to her private exhibition? I didn't have a lot of faith in the justice system. Everything about our lives paraded before a jury, and to most people we were unacceptable.

One visit a week. A tiny block of time to talk about everything else but the shit hurricane that had shredded our lives. I longed to see her, but I didn't want her there. She trusted me to do my job as her husband, but I failed her, and my only option to protect her from the vileness of this place was to make her stay away from here.

I snorted from my own stupidity. I had little control over Angel in a controlled situation when I was in the same room. A jailbreak had less hurdles than keeping my wife from doing something she really wanted.

Exhaustion eventually claimed me, but my last image before falling asleep wore hooker boots and her bound arms and wrists forced her breasts ripe for my pleasure.

Chapter Thirty-Six
Angel

Four months later

Jordan and I had fought more in the last few months than we had in the whole first year we were married. Most of the time, well, all of the time I was at fault. Frustrated, scared, and sick is a petri dish for a hell of an argument.

Jordan couldn't do anything about the no-bail thing. He wasn't responsible for the trial date which at the time seemed light years away. I know he was both sorry and devastated he couldn't go to my doctors' visits. We argued about knowing the sex of the baby. He didn't want to know, and me with the patience of a puppy, was dying to know.

To think I'd believed the real test of our marriage was BDSM.

I had my dad and Jordan's family there for me. They brought me food, cleaned our condo, and any other task I didn't feel up to doing. Which was pretty much everything. The baby's room had a total of one item—a rocking chair that had belonged to Jordan's mom. The bed and dresser remained untouched. I had no baby clothes, no bibs, no diapers, nothing.

Sabrina called me every day and stayed on the line while I puked my guts out. Once the morning sickness subsided, she called me every day to talk and nag me about the baby shower she wanted to plan. She tried not to talk about her and Cameron, but I knew from the tone of her voice, she was crazy happy with her new life. Chicago suited them.

I had constant admonishment to eat. "You need to eat for the baby." "To have a healthy baby, you have to be healthy." I agreed with everything they were saying. Both our families were trying to help. I understood, but not a one of them understood my situation or the feelings of desolation hanging over the uncertainty of my future with my husband.

Our fate, our future depended on twelve people.

The day had arrived.

Chapter Thirty-Seven
Angel

Nearly five months had passed since he'd worn a suit. I had given Luescher my favorite of his, a deep navy color, white shirt and the pale blue tie. The whole thing needed altered I was sure. With every jail visit, I'd noticed more and more weight dropping from his trim body.

I'd been too nervous to eat breakfast. While I knew this trial would last for several days, I convinced myself day one had to go well. Luescher didn't request. He informed me no matter if, even if I was angry with Jordan, I must be in the courtroom every day as a show of complete and unwavering support. He must have gotten wind of our arguments. No worries there. Nothing short of being dead would have kept me away from the proceedings.

He had gone over detail after detail, the prosecution's evidence, the jury list, the background of Judge Talbot, and the entire witness list. When I heard him read off Cameron's name as a character witness, I thought my hearing was going.

I'd pinched the skin on my forearm multiple times until red splotches appeared. Surely, I'd heard him wrong so I asked if Jordan knew, and how did Cameron get on the list? Luescher told me Cameron had come to him and Jordan had the same reaction as I did.

I had four offers to drive me to court. Bri, my dad, Jordan's parents, and his sister. Bri was driving down from Chicago, but much to her parents' dismay, she decided to stay with me. She admitted being around her parents was uncomfortable given she and I shared the same secret…although I'd been outed and not the way I ever thought it would happen. Sabrina however, was still well below the BDSM radar, and her parents had not made the connection between me, Jordan, and Cameron. Not that her parents disliking me was anything new, but now, she informed me, her parents had come out and said, "I told you so," about me being a slut. Only, the word they used was "harlot." I didn't know anyone used "harlot" since Jesus's day, and they were mistaken about me. No money ever changed hands. I worked cheap—requiring only chocolate, orgasm, and an occasional pair of shoes. Bri and I had a tension busting and well-needed laugh over the phone.

On the day of the trial, I chose Allessia to drive me to court. I'd had little opportunity to spend much time with her. She and Jordan were fraternal twins, but they shared many identical physical traits minus a penis on her and boobs on Jordan.

The similarities didn't end at the visible. My jaw hit the floor when Jordan told me Alessia was a Domme. I was fascinated and tried to pump him for information until he showed me the "enough" face.

The ride to court wasn't the place for inquiries into her life, and my mind had other things to process. We had a pleasant conversation but danced around the subject of the day.

When I stepped from the car, a brisk autumn gust of wind nearly blew my dress and coat high enough to flash the crowd waiting to get a seat in the "bondage trial" so named by media outlets. I'd only recently begun wearing maternity clothes. I showed enough, people realized I was pregnant. Our attorney said a pregnant wife could help win over a jury by displaying normalcy. Even Luescher didn't get it.

We were normal.

As I walked into the courtroom, the hairs on my body sizzled to attention from the electric mood in the room. Even in a city with a metro area well over a million people, the popularity of Jordan's case had turned into a circus sideshow. Alessia and I were the last of our group to arrive. Bri moved to allow me to sit between her and my dad. Both of them clasped one of my hands. The warmth of theirs did nothing to ease the glacial feel of my own.

Jordan and I used to lie in bed watching news programs about crimes—murders, robberies, scams. We'd analyze every move, action, and evidence and figure out where the perpetrator went wrong. We'd watched so many, we joked that we had figured out how to commit the perfect crime.

Never once had it occurred one day we'd be fighting for our own futures.

I glanced around the room to see another group of people staring our way or more so I believed at me. The woman with the deadliest expression resembled Jessica. Her mother I assumed. A younger man sat next to her holding her hand. Maybe he was the boyfriend she'd wanted to bring into the room.

Strangers.

We were all strangers brought together by a common thread with each side pulling as hard as they could to yank the thread from the others' grasp. My non-filtered refractory side wanted nothing more than to get in the woman's face and explain exactly how much of a low-life her daughter was. But the compassionate side understood she'd lost her daughter in a violent way and was convinced by the police my husband committed the reprehensible act.

My body ached from tamping down the urge to stand up and scream how unfair this whole thing was. Jordan wasn't a murderer. He was everything kind and honorable. I still harbored a little anger because he didn't tell me about his overtime work, but in the grand scheme of fighting for one's life, I considered the indiscretion a pimple on the ass of survival.

All the independent conversations in the room converged into one hovering buzz, indistinguishable, but loud enough to give me a pounding headache. My mind crawled into a tiny compartment where everything was perfect and this was but a nightmare.

"Emma. Emma." My dad nudged my leg as he spoke. I emerged from my happy cocoon as I spotted Jordan walking into the room escorted by two officers. I chose the suit because I loved how he looked when he came from the bedroom…strong, confident, ready, and incredibly handsome.

Oh my God.

He'd lost so much more weight than I thought. Still handsome, but his face unreadable, out of body until he glanced my way, and our eyes locked.

He winked.

The simple gesture caressed me in this rainbow of love stronger than anything I'd ever experienced. My entire body tingled as if he'd touched me when we were in the cabin. We were having one of those moments when time stopped and no one else mattered. A discreet smile tugged at his lips as his gaze traveled lower. I followed the path and realized my right hand now rested on my growing belly.

A sudden wave of fear choked me. *What if they get it wrong?*

Jordan turned his attention to Luescher who whispered something, and then I heard the bailiff, "All rise for the Honorable Judge Sharon Talbot."

Chapter Thiry-Eight
Jordan

Nerves controlled my life, and I hadn't eaten for two days. The stress drained every ounce of energy I once had until the moment I saw Angel sitting in the courtroom. A sudden rush of adrenaline my soul needed shot through me. I'd told her I didn't want her there while the prosecutor painted us degenerates. She shouldn't have to be a target, but Luescher said her attendance would be very helpful. While I knew he meant Angel's presence could help my case, the very second I saw her with her hand touching her stomach...our baby, I longed to kiss her stomach and meet my son or daughter.

Even with the more than normal makeup on her face, Angel's exterior screamed tired—no exhausted. Apprehension replaced the mischievous seductiveness in her eyes. She gave me a smile, but behind the calm façade she projected in the courtroom, she was afraid. I knew. I knew because I understood everything about her, and Angel didn't handle stress very well. Stressful didn't even begin to describe our lives right now, and I could do nothing for her.

My one saving grace came in the form of a letter from Mr. Levendar. He apologized for distancing himself and the company from me and said he appreciated my cooperation. My attorney told him

Angel was pregnant, and Mr. Levendar said he would personally pay to maintain our health insurance until the baby was born. I didn't know whether he felt guilty, sorry, or ashamed, but nonetheless, I welcomed the gesture. All of our finances went to Luescher and keeping the bills paid, and the money wouldn't last much longer.

I'd had my issues with Sabrina, but she'd never wavered in her support since my arrest even standing up to her parents when they emphatically decreed she had to cut her ties with such morally corrupted individuals. Their daughter seemed to be enjoying the morally corrupt life, and Cameron rated higher on the depraved scale than I did. Watching Sabrina and Angel's dad sandwich Angel between them spoke volumes of how much we all loved her.

My dad slipped his hand into my mom's seeming to signal her of my arrival. When her tear-reddened eyes met mine, her lip quivered and my heart broke. I'd handed them the blindside of the century. Now, they had to wake up every day and walk among people they'd known for years all while many of their *friends* whispered about the sensational details of the shit storm I'd blow in on.

I knew Lessi didn't care. Lessi didn't give a rat's ass about what anyone thought. She kept her personal life quiet but never shied away from telling people to fuck off. Anyone who ever questioned Lessi regretted they did.

I assumed the people sitting on the opposite side of the room were Jessica's family. A man, woman, and another young woman sat together, but one other person with them followed my every motion as I sat down at the defense's table. In his twenties probably, the guy caught my attention because of his intent stare. Our scans of the room connected and locked onto each other. A subtle lift of an eyebrow and hint of a smirk agitated me. Then I remembered Luescher's directions. Be very careful about the emotions displayed. Agitation and anger would not assist my defense.

My assessment of the audience crashed to a halt when the bailiff announced the judge's arrival. In a few more minutes, my dissected private life went before public scrutiny.

So it began.

Chapter Thirty-Nine
Angel

In my head I heard Jordan, "Angel, breathe. You have to breathe." But I couldn't. Every muscle in my chest froze as I watched the prosecutor stand, button his deep navy suit jacket, and approach the jury. Every eye in the room followed his movement.

Glen Evans appeared years younger than Mr. Luescher, but he carried himself with confidence and authority. With receding sandy-brown hair, Evans was attractive, though I wouldn't have said handsome. Still, he commanded attention. Mr. Luescher had told me Evans had a high conviction rate, and I understood how his presence likely played a part. My stomach rolled in trepidation as I waited for him to speak.

"Men and women of the jury." He paused eyeing each of the seven women and five men seated. "Thank you for your service...a noble job. And one I hope you won't take lightly, for a family is grieving the loss of a daughter, sister, and fiancée.

Fiancée? She said he was her boyfriend, and I didn't see a ring on her finger.

"Jessica Forner was an up and coming writer of note. She was a hard worker looking for her big break...her story. The one that would get her a better life and more stable career." He prowled to the middle of the room." She was a sweet young woman who got

177

mixed up with the wrong people and paid the ultimate price."

Emphasizing "wrong people," Evans first cast his regard to the jury, but ended the sentence with an outstretched hand and fingers leading directly to Jordan.

What the fuck?

A strong wide hand tightened on my thigh. My dad knew me well, but I wouldn't jeopardize Jordan by speaking, moving or doing anything the jury could use against him. Every muscle, nerve, and cell wanted to throw a hammer at the guy because the woman he was talking about and the one we encountered were two different people.

"Why would this good-looking man," he again pointed to Jordan. "He is handsome, don't you think? Why would a man who had everything going for him, feel the need and be so desperate that he *brutally* took the life of this young woman?"

Evans whipped from facing Jordan to move to the jury box and placed his hands across the rail. He leaned in as if he were about to tell them a secret. "I'll tell you why. I'll you why Jordan Caldera went to Jessica's apartment, bound her in rope and strangled her."

A silence hung heavy in the room.

"Jordan Caldera's idyllic life had a very, very dark side."

I glanced down our row of family. My dad still grasped my thigh, but his face remained stoic. Jordan's dad equaled his expression, but his mom's ashen face made me fear she'd faint. In one sentence, Evans completely nullified everything Allessia and I explained to Anthony and Jenny about our BDSM lives.

Evans paced in front of the jury, not in a nervous

way, but so everyone had to follow his movement and listen to every fucking word. "You see, Mr. Caldera and his wife lived a BDSM life. Do you know what those letters stand for?"

Pace. Pace. Pace. Fucking stop it.

"Research tells me Bondage, Domination, Sadism, Masochism." He paused. "Bondage, Domination, Sadism, and Masochism."

Even when I didn't really understand the life, I never had feedings of disgust. The words spit from Evans' mouth like a vile piece of rotting meat, and I couldn't stop myself from turning my head to Jordan. My thumb and forefinger circled the thin silver disk of my collar, and the vibration of my pounding heart thundered through my fingers.

With almost indistinguishable effort, he mouthed, "I love you." From across the room and with no way to touch me, my husband reached my fearful soul with his gentle spirit.

Evans knew nothing about us, and spewed his judgmental rhetoric to the jury and audience of voyeurs. "This couple are part a band of deviants who regularly engage in sexual acts no God-fearing person could imagine. Women who kneel to their masters and men who whip them into submission if they disobey."

Some on the jury seemed horrified—others interested and intrigued. In no way could I gauge the air of opinion in the room. My fists curled. My knee didn't bob. No, no nerves now. I remembered to breathe because my deep breaths kept me from screaming. No, I didn't understand at first what he wanted, but I'm the one who begged him to use the flogger and crop. All my choices.

"What did Jessica Forner have to do with this?" With Shakespearian grandeur, Evans advanced closer to Jordan. "You see, Jessica was writing a story about Mr. and Mrs. Caldera…at their request, I might add. But somewhere, somehow along the line, things got ugly. Because Jessica isn't here to tell us, we don't know exactly why. Maybe, the Calderas wanted Jessica to join them in their dungeon of sexual depravity and she refused."

How could he be allowed to say those lies?

He flittered back and forth across his stage telling a tale of two people I didn't know. We weren't those people, and I could do nothing but watch the performance and the others riveted to his every word.

"That, ladies and gentlemen, is what we will do."

What? Fuck I must have tuned out.

"We will show the brutal how and why Mr. Caldera murdered Jessica Forner because not only does she deserve justice, but her family deserves the truth."

The truth. Not one word he spoke about us was the truth. He painted us sexual freaks. Thirty minutes into the trial and my heart sank to a depth I didn't know existed.

Chapter Forty
Jordan

God Damn. If I'd sat on the jury, Mr. Caldera would be on his way to prison. Luescher had said Evans had charisma.

The entire room remained silent. My own rapid and shallow breathing seemed to broadcast throughout the court. Had it been that loud? Or had the surrealism of the situation enhanced my senses to a ridiculous level.

I glanced to the jury and on to the judge and then the spectators. They stared at me, but not as if I made an ungodly sound, but rather committed an ungodly act. An emerging despair weighed heavily on my shoulders.

Luescher made his own grand entrance. He stood in slow motion while he smoothed his suit and tugged at the sleeves. He moved with grace and confidence to the jury box.

"Thank you, Mr. Evans, for that gripping story." A huge smile spilled across his face lifting his amused eyes. "And men and women of the jury, that's all it was…a story."

Hope upon hope.

He shook a pointed index finger before facing Evans. "That's not completely true. Mr. and Mrs. Caldera do practice…as consenting adults, acts of BDSM, in the privacy of their home. However, Mr. Evans' melodramatic description could lead a person to believe what the prosecution has garnered from a few websites." He leaned in to the jury resting a forearm on the rail. "And we know the internet is gospel for information."

He popped up and pointed again. "Oh, yes, the other truth. Jessica Forner was murdered. However, not by my client."

"Mr. Caldera is a hard working professional, and I will use the cliché because it's true. Jordan Caldera has not received even a parking ticket in his entire life."

Luescher had his own form of performance, inserting a dramatic pause. He crossed his arms and stood like a statue until everyone in the room paid him attention.

"Not even a parking ticket." He unfolded his arms in reverse order and then touched his fingertips together before drawing them to his mouth. "Think about that. Why would a man like that murder a reporter? So what if she revealed Mr. and Mrs. Caldera's identities. They weren't doing anything illegal. We have two consenting married adults, having sex, maybe a little left of center. He couldn't be fired for it. Well, unless he engaged in such activity on company time on company property."

Luescher didn't pace the room like Evans. He used the space as his stage for his own brand of soliloquy. "We welcome the prosecution's case. Welcome it. Because best case, their evidence is completely circumstantial and there's very little of it."

He moved again to stand in front of the jury. "You're not here to convict. You're here to find the truth."

In but a few minutes, Harry Luescher had nullified the damage I believed Evan's opening statement created.

For the rest of the day, the prosecution paraded witnesses before the jury—mostly the police officers on the scene, crime scene technicians, and the detective who arrested me. Evans showed crime scene photos on a screen. They included unremarkable shots of her apartment until he displayed the one of her open laptop. On the screen was the story about Angel and me. She'd opened the document the night she'd been killed. The enlarged pictures on the screen displayed our names, as if the whole room consisted of a collection of elderly people with failing eyesight and hearing loss. Evans made sure everyone knew what they were seeing.

"If anyone's having trouble reading what's in this picture, let me assist. "Jordan and Emma Caldera are a normal couple. Normal being a relative term. Normal meaning tightly binding your wife to complete immobilization and denying sexual release."

"Objection." Luescher jumped to his feet as I swallowed hard hearing how she judged our lives in a few carefully chosen words.

"This is circumstantial. There's no proof Miss Forner was telling the truth."

"Overruled." Judge Talbot eyed Luescher, paused until he sat and gave a slight nod for Evans to continue.

Luescher leaned to my ear. "Don't look away. Don't look at your wife. Listen like you're hearing it for the first time."

I couldn't stop my brow from jumping in frustration. Sitting in silence while someone is destroying you was never part of my skillset. "I am hearing it for the first time. I've never seen that document." I said in the lowest voice I could muster.

It's so hard to whisper when every instinct is pushing you to get loud, fast.

At least the judge stopped him from reading the whole thing. Some members of the jury squirmed in their seats when Evans read detailed accounts of kink scenes. Interesting, or infuriating the better word choice, because the words he read were complete fiction. She made up extreme depictions of BDSM neither Angel nor I had ever engaged in—dangerous and ridiculous things.

I sat with my jaw clenched so hard, my teeth hurt. Fury raged and rolled making my muscles exhausted and my stomach weak. Luescher must have picked up on my demeanor for he passed me a note.

We will have our turn.

Little comfort. Evans displayed a smart phone and announced the item as entered into evidence. He swiped through the phone, touched the screen, and placed the phone on a small table close to the jury box. When I heard the recording of Jessica and I having our discussion, my heart sank even lower.

If the story and recording wasn't damning enough, the next prosecution witness was. I knew what he'd have to say.

The DNA.

When the expert stated my DNA appeared underneath Jessica's fingernails, he raised the curtain for Evans' short but dramatic conclusion. "You are saying Mr. Caldera's DNA was found on Jessica's body?"

"Yes."

Evans' attention shifted to the jury. "There you have it. The DNA found underneath Jessica's fingernails belongs to Jordan Caldera, proving the two struggled before he bound her wrists and wrapped even more rope around her neck, slowly tightening until Jessica lost consciousness and died from strangulation. And let me add." He raised his index finger. "It takes roughly three to five minutes for someone to die from strangulation."

"Objection. This is speculation. Mr. Evans was not present."

"Sustained. Mr. Evans," said the judge, "you need not be so dramatic."

Luescher seized the opportunity to question the expert on cross-examination. "Was Mr. Caldera's DNA found anywhere else in the apartment?"

"No."

"Was DNA other than Miss Forner's found in the apartment."

"Yes, her boyfriend's."

"Her boyfriend. Would that be Derrek Cooper?"

"Yes."

"Is this DNA specific to Miss Forner's apartment?"

"Meaning?"

"Could Mr. Caldera's DNA have gotten under her fingernails in another location…or perhaps on another day?"

"Yes, it's possible."

"No, more questions, your Honor."

He scored the biggest victory of the day for me. Not enough, but by then I'd have taken anything.

****

Each day, when I walked into the courtroom, my stolen glances of my Angel rejuvenated my drive and my soul. By the end of each day, I'd almost convinced myself I'd killed Jessica—that I was guilty.

Angel sat in the same seat every day flanked by my family and hers. She appeared everything she wasn't…conservative, demure, and quiet. I knew every curve and secret, wicked, and glorious realm of carnality she possessed and used. Since this trial began, I also witnessed the subtle hints she was hanging onto a whispery thread of sanity. Her dark eyes were void of sensual mischief—replaced by dull hues and redness. While her belly displayed her pregnancy, her collarbone was more prominent and her face slimmer.

And her collar rested loosely at the base of her neck.

Like me, she'd lost a lot of weight. I'd lost so much, I had to ask Luescher to poke another hole in my belt to keep my pants from slipping from my hips.

When would it be our turn?

Chapter Forty-One
Jordan

Our day.

Throughout the trial, I'd made notes for Luescher to counter attack. Things I knew to be untrue, incorrect statements, and of course the painting of the BDSM community as sexual predators and deviants.

I opened my notebook to show him a few more items when Sabrina handed him a note. Luescher read the brief note and smiled.

"What is it?" I asked.

"We may have our ace." He handed me the note. As I read Sabrina's handwriting, for the first time in months, my stress dropped a half a percent. A glimmer of unknown hope.

"It's not for sure yet, but fingers crossed."

Luescher started by presenting evidence of everything I hadn't done—no criminal record, clean driving record, no sexual harassment suits. He went on to show a couple of civic awards, a volunteer award, and charity work. He listed things I'd worked on over the years and never gave a thought one day they might mean something.

Then he called Cameron to the stand.

A lot of heads turned and women smiled when he walked to the front of the court.

The bailiff swore him in, and my biggest opponent

became a guy to testify about my character.

Luescher began. "Mr. Terry. How long have you known and how do you know Mr. Caldera?"

"I've known Jordan about six years. We are colleagues at work, occasional rivals and sometimes run in the same social circles.

My jaw clenched to keep from expressing my shock over his words. Cameron was on the verge of outing himself in public. Well, his dinners with the future in-laws would be interesting. "What kind of man is Mr. Caldera?"

"Well." Cameron stared straight my way before he cast his sight around the room and stopped on the jury. "Jordan's a hard worker, a loyal worker. He, uh, puts in a lot of hours. He's good to those who work for him."

"And again. How long have you been friends?"

A smile tugged at the corners of Cameron's mouth. "Oh, we are not friends."

Luescher faced the jury before asking what he already knew. "Not friends. But, yet you're here as a character witness."

"That's right."

"Earlier, you said the word 'rivals.' What did you mean by that?"

Like he was at cocktail party, Cameron crossed his legs and relaxed more into the witness chair. "Even though we handle different aspects of clients and the business, there is still opportunity to *one up* each other on occasion. We're both competitive people and there is sometimes friction between us."

I could tell Luescher loved Cameron. Cocky bastards both of them.

"Friction. How did Mr. Caldera handle the friction

between you? Did you ever come to physical violence?"

"Jordan always walked away. We've never gotten into a physical fight." You would have thought testifying was his job. Not one hesitant moment. He didn't even sound rehearsed. Which I'm sure he wasn't. Cameron was never at a loss for words.

I kept scanning the room while he became the Pied Piper. He mesmerized the room. He captivated his captive audience. And yeah, fuck, I realized they should be staring. He was a fucking articulate, charismatic, and handsome man.

"And do you know Mr. Caldera's wife, Emma?"

Both Angel and I straightened with surprise. Why the hell did he bring Angel into this? I shot a quick glance her way, and she seemed to have the same reaction of disbelief.

"I do know Emma. I'm engaged to her best friend Sabrina, and prior to that I'd flirt outrageously with her whenever I had the opportunity."

"Why would you flirt with another man's wife?"

His shoulders shook with amusement. "It was fun, and I knew it would anger Jordan." He paused and passed his glint across the room. "And I knew I never stood a chance with her, because Jordan is a good man."

"Thank you, Mr. Terry."

Cameron nodded and started to rise.

"I have a few questions for Mr. Terry." Evans approached the witness stand with confidence, and I didn't like the way he studied both Cameron and me.

"Mr. Terry. Earlier in your statement, you said both you and Mr. Caldera ran in the same social circles.

What did you mean by that?"

I detected the tiniest of movement across Cameron's throat as he swallowed. He realized he'd made a mistake. No one else would. Good PR people had an answer for everything. Great PR people never let anyone see them flinch. That asshole was great.

"We have mutual friends."

But Evans was good too. Cocky bastard against cocky bastard. "Mutual friends. Would those mutual friends happen to be in the BDSM community?"

"Yes."

A low rumble of murmurs echoed in the room. I was quite sure in many peoples' eyes, Cameron's credibility crashed and burned.

"So, Mr. Terry, you're one of those people? Wouldn't you say anything to make your people seem respectable?"

For a moment, I forgot I was on trial for my life and became fully engaged waiting for Cameron to scale the wall and decimate the arrogant king. I knew the man well enough to notice the telltale signs he was about to release the arrows pinning the sanctimonious dick to the wall. Yep, Cameron was not going to defend, he was going to attack.

"My people, Mr. Evans. I'm quite sure if we examined Jordan's and my list of friends in our group, you won't find one person who has drug issues, alcohol issues, or domestic violence issues. You won't find a one of them on a sexual predator list. Not one of them is a child molester. What you will find are adults enjoying healthy, consenting sexual relationships who are attorneys, teachers, social workers, chefs, and a hundred other respectable careers. You'll find people with very deep faith. You'll find people who will jump into a rushing river to save a puppy."

He stopped and drew in a slow, deep breath. "Can you say that about all of your friends?"

Evan's face went from red to white. "No more questions, your Honor."

"Mr. Terry, you may step down," said Judge Talbot.

I still didn't like him, but everyone needed someone like Cameron on his or her side.

Chapter Forty-Two
Angel

My jaw hit the floor after listening to Cameron's response to the prosecutor's attack. Just because people didn't' talk about kink in open conversations didn't mean plenty of people had a little edge to their sex life.

Fuck. Fuck.

Sabrina's parents would never have been in the courtroom, but now with all the media coverage, they would know about her and Cameron. I slipped my hand into hers and squeezed. Her stricken expression made me want to hug her for hours, but not now, not here.

She gave me a weak and feigned smile. "It's okay," she said. "I'm sure at some point I'd have to tell them. Mom keeps pressuring me to dump you…more than usual."

I almost giggled at her add on.

"I won't make the mistake of being judgmental again. I lost you and almost lost Cameron. I'm adulting now."

"You picked an interesting subject to adult about." I squeezed her hand harder.

"Besides, I don't live here anymore. I love Chicago, and you'll have to come visit, a lot."

"I will." I feared my visits would be only the baby and me. "What did you give Luescher?"

"I don't want to say unless it works out."

I didn't like cryptic, and I liked it even less when I was the one who didn't know what was going on.

I continued to hold her hand until the judge concluded proceedings were over for the day. She drove us home, fixed grilled cheese sandwiches and tomato soup for dinner. Comfort food for a cold stressful day. Wine was more my comfort food but the pregnancy thing and all.

In the evenings, I tried to stay up and talk with Sabrina. She'd stopped her life to watch over me, and I loved her for everything she had done. But the only real solace I found was in our bedroom.

At night, I wrapped in the blankets and talked to Jordan. I never talked about what happened in court. I talked liked we talked at the end of any other day or when we'd finished a scene. Jordan always wanted to talk. I wanted a silent snuggle. My whole body ached with the pain of not having him with me. I missed him. I would have given anything for those talks I didn't want to have, and I began to hate the silence.

At the very moment I believed I'd lost the little remaining strength to function, I'd hear Jordan in his way telling me to hang on. Little kicks from inside reminded me of the precious life I carried.

I didn't have the choice to give up.

Chapter Forty-Three
Jordan

"Your Honor, we have new evidence and a new witness for Mr. Caldera's case."

Stunned kind of described Evan's reaction. "The prosecution will need time to review these changes."

The day ended before even beginning. Judge Talbot called a recess until the next day. My opportunity to see Angel gone before it even began. I should have been happy about Lueschers' ace, but seeing my wife every day kept me going each day.

I'd close my eyes and smell the sweetness of her hair as the wild curls tangled in my fingers. With a fistful of twisted hair, I'd draw her head back until her eyes met mine and saw my need to devour every inch of her. My eyes snapped open. I heard a baby cry, but babies weren't allowed in court. My attention locked on to Angel, and her hands would be resting on her stomach and our baby.

I had to win this. We had to win this.

The next morning Luescher went to work. He called attention to the screen and pushed a button on a remote.

"This video was recorded at Koffees coffee shop two days before Jessica was found dead. If you'll look to the top right corner, you'll see Jessica sitting at a booth." He fast-forwarded for a few seconds. "Now, see the man in the suit approaching the table? That is Jordan Caldera. He brings two cups to the table, removes his jacket, pushes up his shirt sleeves and sits across from her, and it looks like they're talking." He turned to the jury. "Since we can't hear what is being said, I'm going to fast forward to the part where Jessica leaves." He pressed a button and we saw animated hand motions until he abruptly stopped the video. "There."

Jessica and I froze in time. So long ago, but not really.

"Do you see what Mr. Caldera is doing? He's taking hold of her bag. I'm going to start the tape again."

I watched myself with the death grip on her bag and remembered every word we spoke. I remembered thinking it was the first time I truly ever hated someone.

"There. Right there." He stopped the tape. "What's Miss Forner doing?"

Some of the jury members nodded.

"Yes, she's scratching Mr. Caldera's forearm with her fingernails. Which would place his DNA under her nails. If she didn't wash underneath her fingernails, that would explain why Mr. Caldera's DNA appeared on her body, and if you remember, nowhere else in the apartment or on her body was the presence of Jordan Caldera's DNA."

Luescher returned to the table, but he left the video frozen on the screen. I glanced over to Angel to see her whispering to Sabrina and smiling. Sabrina was the one who noticed the video camera in Koffee's. Two people I'd really disliked had presented me with hope.

"The defense has one more witness. I'd like to call Preston Graham to the stand.

Shit, Preston.

Preston had spent a fair amount of his life as a bouncer until he'd discovered a honey hole.

"Mr. Graham, what do you do for a living?"

"I own Heaven's Boat Yacht Club."

"Could you elaborate please?"

"Yes, sir."

This man whose livelihood depended on secrecy, was about to spill.

"The Yacht Club is a private, secret adult club."

"So what goes on at your club?"

Preston licked his lips and sipped the water provided. "Some people have different sexual needs, desires, fetishes and our club is an outlet for them."

"So you have a sex club?"

"In a manner of speaking, but not all fetishes lead to sex."

Mimicking Evans, Luescher paced the floor, but kept the focus on Preston. "Is Mr. Caldera a member there?"

"No, sir, but he has access to the club through another member and he sometimes brings guests to the club."

"So on the night in question, was Mr. Caldera at the Yacht Club?"

Preston and my eyes met, and he nodded. "Yes. Jordan brought two men, one older, one younger around nine p.m. They left around one a.m."

"Does or has Mr. Caldera engaged in the offerings of the club?"

Something between a snort and humph left Preston's mouth. I hoped he didn't use his nickname for me. Boy Scout.

"Jordan does nothing but sign them in and out. The in-between time he sits in the lounge drinking a soda or coffee and works on his laptop or sits and talks to me about how incredible his wife is."

A collective giggle spread throughout the courtroom, and I watched Angel go through a few shades of pink and red.

"Did Mr. Caldera at any time leave the club before one a.m.?"

"No, sir. I was present the entire time, and he never moved."

"So Mr. Caldera doesn't participate, drinks no alcohol, and on that particular night left the club around one a.m., and the surveillance cameras at his condo shows him arriving home at one forty a.m. Miss Forner's apartment is seven point three miles from the Yacht Club's location at 1172 Beaumont Ave."

Luescher walked to the table, retrieved a piece of paper from a folder, and held the paper for the jury to see. "Says here Jessica Forner's time of death was likely after nine p.m.

"With most of the travel area within the city, seven miles could take a while, and the odds of him slipping in and out unseen, dropping off his clients, and arriving at his own home some forty minutes after he left the club? Well, the odds are highly unlikely Mr. Caldera made a detour to tie up and strangle Miss Forner."

Preston motioned for attention.

"Mr. Graham, you have something else?"

"We don't serve alcohol of any kind at the club. Keeps the stupid level way down."

Another wave of laughter rolled through.

"Your witness, Mr. Evans."

Evans pressed nonexistent wrinkles from his sleeve as he approached Preston. "Mr. Graham, what do you have to gain from this testimony? More clients? More money?"

"Quite the opposite. I'll have to move the club. Between finding a new location, moving everything inside to the new place, and notifying club members, coming here will cost me quite a chunk of money."

Evans fixed a confused expression on his face. "And why would you have to move?"

"After today, we will no longer be a secret and the publicity of this trial will bring a hoard of curiosity clowns. I'm here because Jordan's best alibis are either too holier than thou or too chicken shit to come forward. And he's a good guy who doesn't deserve what's happened to him. We have high-end clients, some of whom *may* even be people you know. Let me rephrase…are people you know. Publicity is bad for my business, so I'll have to move. Don't worry, I'll notify *everyone*."

Bested by a witness once again. I believe steam blew from Evans' ears.

The next day closing arguments began. Instead of pushing the sexual deviant angle as he did in the beginning, Evans portrayed me as someone who was terrified of losing everything if his hidden life became public. He narrated a plausible reason for her murder and something the jury might buy into.

All of the testimony in my defense seemed to fade under Evans' passionate reasoning. And once again, I was thankful for Luescher getting to grandstand last. And I was thankful he countered every damning word Evans had to say.

Chapter Forty-Four
Angel

Three days.

Three days and the jury still hadn't reached a verdict.

They had their instructions and everything they needed. Going into the first day, I had confidence Jordan would be going home with me, but once two days had passed, my nerves rambled throughout my body, stabbing my heart and emptying my stomach. I became afraid I was damaging our baby, but I couldn't help my state of mind.

"Mr. Luescher, I don't understand what's taking so long. Is there anything else you could have done to prove Jordan's innocence?"

"Emma, I wasn't trying to prove innocence, I was trying to create doubt, and I believe I did that."

Doubt.

So either the majority believed him innocent or there were holdouts for guilty or the other way around. I didn't care for any scenario but the one where we got our lives back.

The word came at two thirty-seven and we had to be in court in two hours to hear the verdict. Now that we'd soon have an answer, a huge dose of reality clawed at my stomach. Before, everything sat in limbo, and I carried on in a make believe world. The reading of the verdict would change everything.

Like every day since the trial began, we went through the routine of beginning court, except, I knew this session had but a few minutes.

Jordan entered and as we locked onto each other, he gave me a wink, and I nearly burst into tears. *Did he believe this was good-bye?*

Judge Talbot described what would happen and made a point to lecture the audience once the verdict was read, to maintain the proper courtroom decorum. Judge Talbott instructed Jessica's family to exit the courtroom first, and then she would dismiss Jordan's side ten minutes later. The bailiff handed her the paper announcing the balance of our lives.

I stopped breathing, and battled the need to vomit.

"Will the defendant rise?"

Jordan stood and buttoned his suit coat. Old habits.

She began to read in the silent room, and I closed my eyes. "In the case of the state verses Jordan Caldera in the murder of Jessica Forner, the jury finds the defendant…not guilty."

Not guilty. *Not guilty.* Had I heard correctly? *Not fucking guilty.*

I opened my eyes to see Jordan hugging Mr. Luescher. Not guilty.

Judge Talbot thanked the jury and turned to Jordan. "Mr. Caldera, you are free to go."

Free to go.

Free to go home with me.

Free to be a dad.

The modicum of decorum I clung to, crumbled away, and I shoved past everyone exiting the courtroom until I latched on to the man I hadn't touched in months.

"Oh my God, I have you back." My arms locked so tightly around his neck, I may have cut off his oxygen supply. For a time we said nothing, but bound ourselves together stricter than any rope. He smelled of industrial soap, and his body had changed. His defined muscles had shrunk, and the hard, toned chest absorbed instead of supported me. I didn't care. Those things would return, but even if they didn't, I had my world back.

The stress and joy of the last several months broke me. An uncontrollable wave of sobs racked my body, but Jordan didn't attempt to wipe my tears nor encourage me to stop. His own body trembled with quiet tears.

My selfish side wanted everyone to leave us alone, but I wasn't the only one who needed to touch him. Unhooking my arms from Jordan's neck, I stepped aside for Anthony, Jenny, and Alessia. My dad's hands rubbed up and down my upper arms.

Not to be left out, Sabrina kissed my cheek and hugged me all while fielding a call to I assume was Cameron. "It's over, Jaynie, and you have your life back. Now you can be a mom like you should and things will be back to normal."

As much as I wanted to believe her, I doubted Jordan and I could pick up where we left off months ago. Too much had changed.

We'd changed.

Chapter Forty-Five
Jordan

Two weeks later

I didn't watch any television in jail, and now with the whole fifty-five inch TV to myself, I still couldn't watch. Everything coming across the picture annoyed me. Too loud, too bright, too stupid, and plain too much. I even gave up on the basketball game. Everything seemed so superficial.

Rubbing an itchy eye, my hand brushed the beard rapidly growing again on my face. Angel didn't like it, but she didn't say anything. In fact, she didn't say much of anything contrary to me. She walked on eggshells when I was around, and I had nowhere to go, so I was around twenty-four, seven.

I supposed the stress of the trial and being pregnant had taken a physical toll on her as well. Every afternoon, Angel slept for two to three hours, leaving me alone to ponder a non-future.

In the middle of the third time through the channels, the doorbell rang. I jumped from the sofa to answer before the noise woke Angel.

Cameron Terry stood in my doorway.

"Terry."

"Caldera."

I still didn't like this guy but… "I never said thank you, and I'm sorry, but I appreciate every word you said, even if you didn't mean them, and that's okay."

I backed away to allow him to enter. Dressed in a deep brown suit, Cameron had somewhere to be. *Must be nice.*

"What are you doing here? Shouldn't you be in Chicago?"

He waltzed over toward the kitchen island while I flopped to my permanent spot on the sofa.

"Closing on my house today and scheduled a meeting for a potential client…Brian Donovan."

"Baseball player?" I sipped a warm beer. The bottle'd been setting on the floor in front of my feet for hours.

"Yep. You know for a guy who avoided going to prison, you don't seem too happy."

"I'm happy." *As happy as a guy can be in my present position.*

"Look at you." Cameron cross his arms and leaned against the counter. "You got a fuckin' mountain man thing going on with the face. That T-shirt looks like you've slept in it and from the whiff I caught when I came in, when's the last time you showered?"

Crossing my own arms and legs, I put up my shield. "Yes, I'm happy as a fucking clam not to be going to prison. I really am, but the fact is, I have no job and little to no chance of getting a decent job now thanks to the notoriety. I have no means of supporting my wife and soon arriving child. My defense and expenses here cleaned us out financially. We have enough to stay in this place maybe two months, and then an almost thirty-seven year old man gets to move his family in with his parents. Should I go on?"

"You're not going to prison, you asshole."

We glared at one another like lasers trying to fry the retinas.

"The reason I came by other than to visit with Mr. GQ, is to offer you a job, at my company in Chicago."

I narrowed my eyes trying to figure out his angle. "A job? We don't even like each other. Why would you want me to work for you?"

"Well." Cameron went to my fridge, opened it, and snatched a bottle of water.

What the fuck?

"Well," he said twisting off the plastic cap and taking a quick sip. "Two reasons really. One, face the fact that Sabrina and I are getting married, she, and Emma are best friends. And two, we may not care that much for each other, but the truth is you, Caldera are damn good. I need someone like you to make my company successful."

He tipped the bottle back for a long drink. "I can set up an advance to get you and Emma up there and settled. It'll take a bit to make the really good money, but once we get things rolling, the opportunities are endless in Chicagoland."

"Cameron." Angel emerged from the bedroom sleepy eyed and yawning. "Is Sabrina with you?"

He shook his head and set the empty bottle on the counter. "No, she had a job interview."

As I stared at Angel's profile, I realized only a short time remained until our baby arrived. Still the only baby item in the other bedroom was the rocker. My mom wanted to give her a shower, but decided to wait until we moved in and had everything under one roof.

One roof. I bounced my head against the back of

the sofa contemplating Terry as my boss. Life really did find more than one way to fuck you.

"Cameron's offered me a job."

"In Chicago?"

"In Chicago."

Immediately, her eyes brightened and she was happy, but her enthusiasm faded and her shoulders slumped.

"Oh. Are you considering it? I mean is that what you'd like?"

No more. I couldn't take anymore of her acquiescing for my benefit. "Tell me what you'd like, Angel."

Her mouth opened, but nothing came out.

"Give me your opinion. What do you think we should do?"

Her eyes darted from me to Cameron and back. "I think we need to take an opportunity and make a new life for ourselves."

She glided over to the sofa and sat next to me. "Jordan, I love your parents, but I don't want to live with them, nor my dad either. I want us to be our own family."

I patted her leg. "When do you want us up there?"

Cameron flashed his dazzler set of teeth. "As soon as possible. You won't regret this."

"I'm sure I'll regret every second you're my boss."

Angel leaned in and whispered. "Maybe now would be a good time to get back in the habit of showering and shaving."

God, I loved this woman.

Epilogue
Jordan

The shore of Lake Michigan in the summer in the city hosted most of our free time. As Angel and I and Frankie in the stroller roamed along the sidewalk with the skyscrapers of Chicago on one side and the sparkling waves of the lake on the other, I'd never been happier.

Money was tight, but in a few years, with the company growing as fast as it was, our income would grow as well. Angel had kept her clientele, which kept us from having to pay childcare if she worked out of the home.

Cameron had given me free rein to control the marketing and I had to admit he wasn't a bad boss. We still had our clashes, but he was willing to listen to every side. He'd hired a few more employees, and we celebrated every new contract with pizza and beer.

With some creative games and outside help, Angel and I had returned to embrace our needs—not as often as we wanted, but Frankie made our lives complete.

"What time is Sabrina picking up Frankie," I asked.

"As soon as I call when we get back." She stopped the stroller and pulled me with her a few steps back. "So what are we doing after she picks him up?"

"Lascivious, new, and hmmm, maybe a little

difficult things." I loved vague, because Angel hated vague.

"What things? Come on, a little hint." She back away from me, but closer to Frankie. "Maybe I won't like it. Maybe I won't do it."

"You'll love it."

She ran her tongue along her lips and then scraped her teeth across her bottom lip. Nothing like getting a woody in public.

"What if I don't do it?"

"You know the agreement. You disobey you pay the consequences. Come on, let's get a hotdog."

"No."

"*No?*"

With arms crossed and legs planted firmly she reiterated. "No, I don't want to."

I'm not sure why I stuffed the little metal lock in my jeans before we left, but I did. I patted my front pocket. "Do you realize what I have in here?"

She eyed my growing crotch.

"Not there, in my pocket."

"And you're going to pull that out in public? You wouldn't."

"I most definitely would."

Angel began fumbling through the diaper bag.

"What are you doing?"

She flashed me her phone. "I was looking for this. I want Sabrina to meet us there instead of having to wait for her."

"Good idea."

Because the next several hours were going to be exquisite and exhausting. She had no idea what was coming.

Anna Hague

About the Author

My career in Sports Journalism spans over twenty-five years. I currently do freelance sports reporting to allow more time for writing. My venture into published romance writing began in 2016, and I live in central Indiana with my husband, three parrots, and two dogs.

~*~

Visit Anna at
http://annahague.com

Angel's Collar

Love Strictly Tested Book One

By Anna Hague

I have it all…until he shows me more.

I didn't intentionally spill wine all over the most beautiful guy in the room, and one look at those icy-blue eyes brings on a major lapse in coherent speech. Jordan Caldera tells me his secret and wants me to join him. This is where my journey into submission begins.

So much about BDSM freaks me out, but at the same time, I can't help but be intrigued. When I imagine Jordan doing those things to me, I can't resist the adventure. Mind-blowing sex aside, my life is changing at an alarming rate and getting very complicated. Between balancing my career and my best friend's concerns, the secrets I'm keeping are killing me.

What am I willing to risk for the new lifestyle I've embraced…and the man I love?

Also Available
from The Wild Rose Press, Inc.
and major retailers.

Revving Her Heart
A Blacke Brothers Novel Book One
By Cadence Vonn

After the sudden death of Allison Lorde's father in a motorcycle accident, she vows never to love a man who rides the beastly machines. But when a memory from her past rides up on his bike, looking all bad-boy sexy, the sweet promise of a shared kiss long ago makes it difficult to deny his steamy seduction.

Nick Blacke's number one passion is motorcycles until the gangly girl he'd kissed as a teen shows up with womanly curves that beckon to be explored. She seems eager to let him and even embraces his penchant for kink, but when he wants more, he realizes revving her engines might be easier than revving her heart.

Thank you for purchasing
this publication of The Wild Rose Press, Inc.

For questions or more
information contact us at
info@thewildrosepress.com.

The Wild Rose Press, Inc.
www.thewildrosepress.com